KING'S CROWN

OIL KINGS - BOOK ONE

MARIE JOHNSTON

LE PUBLISHING

For my Family

CHAPTER 1

endall

I PICKED AT MY HEMLINE. If I had to wait outside my boss's office any longer, I'd unravel the edge and walk away in a frayed hot mess. My phone vibrated, and I looked around. With my family, I couldn't let it go for long.

The coast was clear. I dug it out of my wrap-around dress pocket and looked at the caller. Yep. My youngest brother. His homework was probably late, or he forgot to get his band card signed. Or he needed money for some club. Or he had a band performance he didn't tell anyone about.

It was probably safe to call him back later. He was old enough to know what to do if he missed the bus. Again.

I slipped the phone back in my pocket and twiddled my thumbs, giving my hemline a break. When was this meeting going to happen? Sitting here gave me too much time to think about my roommate situation, which was also my ex-husband situation. We'd been divorced for almost two years, but had devolved into roommates long before that.

We'd fallen into the complacency of sharing a house. I worked days, and he was on nights at the refinery. Most of his free time was spent at the bar watching "the game" that always seemed to be on no matter what season it was. Our lease was up on our rental house in a week, but Darren refused to talk about signing a new one.

I should've saved up for a place of my own, but I'd taken a gamble. Share rent and pay down loans, and I could afford a bigger place.

Who was I kidding. I was only sharing a place so that I didn't have to move back home. *How can you keep this place without my income, Kendall? You know you're going to move back home. It's inevitable and would save you a lot of fucking phone calls.*

I shouldn't have been intimidated by his insecurity when it came to my family. If I had moved home, I would've had a lot more saved up by now.

The foreboding wide panel door to my boss's office opened. Finally.

Mr. Golding peered out, his hound-dog face especially droopy. "Ms. Brinkley, come on in."

I couldn't tell from his demeanor what this meeting was about. Mr. Golding was typically dour, always bemoaning the worst-case scenario. Why he'd chosen the marketing field was a mystery to me, but at least his doom and gloom tone wasn't selling our clients' products. I was.

"Sorry to keep you waiting," he said as he rounded his desk with a sigh. "It's been an unrelenting morning."

That's what he said every day. The only thing that changed was whether it was morning or afternoon.

"No problem." I sat in the no-frills metal chair across from him. The un-upholstered seat had long lost its padding, and he was too cheap to buy a new one. I tried to broach the possibility of a work injury claim if it collapsed under someone, but no dice.

He took his glasses off and huffed out a breath that left his mouth hanging open. I wasn't sure he'd continue until he blinked up at me. "I'm going to come right out and say that we have to let you go. With many of our clients turning to cheaper online competition, our profits have shrunk to the point where I need to downsize. Your position is being dissolved."

I bobbed my head, trying to process what he said. Dissolved? "So where am I going to work? Inquiries?" The mailroom? I'd take anything.

This job was the only thing keeping me from moving back in with my parents. I loved them a lot. They worked hard, to the point of being workaholics, and as the oldest kid, they leaned on me. But if I moved back home, it'd be on the tail of Darren's *I told you so*.

"Outside of this company, Kendall." He smiled, the look hardly transforming his face. He only smiled at bonus time when he explained how much we were worth and then paid us less. "It's just… I prolonged it as long as I can, but during lean times we have to make cuts."

Cuts. I was losing my job. *Shit*. "Why me? I thought my productivity this past year was—"

"It's your education."

"Excuse me?" I had a degree in business administration with a minor in marketing. I didn't major in the eight ways to tap a keg like Terry in public relations. I bet he wasn't getting fired.

He explained like he wasn't tearing my worth down to pennies. "You have a four-year degree, but most of your coworkers have a graduate degree or certificate. While you would think that would make you cheaper to retain, I'm going to need those higher education credentials to level up with the clients we have and attract more."

A graduate degree. I'd wanted one. I had even enrolled. But then I met Darren the last year of college and decided to live a little—which equated to getting a job so we could afford a roof over our heads and pay student loans. I hadn't even been able to move out of Billings after I left Montana State. Now I was almost twenty-nine, losing a damn job because I'd been young and stupid and in love.

"I can give you a good recommendation."

I cocked my head, uncharacteristically letting my irritation run free. "Really? 'Yeah, she was so valuable I laid her off.' Big help there, boss."

His scraggly gray brows popped up. "I mean…"

"Never mind, sorry. Yes, I'd appreciate it."

I gathered what little pride I had left and walked out. I had the whole building to navigate to get back to my desk. My heels didn't make a sound on the carpet tiles. The squares were the ugliest brown I'd ever seen, but then, Mr. Golding had picked it out from a clearance warehouse.

I passed Mary from billing, and she gave me a sunny smile that said she had no clue I was walking the plank.

On my way to my cubicle, I popped into the supply closet. I needed boxes. The shelves were stacked with pen boxes and Wite-Out. My gaze landed on the copier paper.

Perfect. Dumping the reams of paper on to the floor, I emptied two boxes. I ignored the compulsion to organize the reams. Someone who was getting paid could do it.

My cubicle mate, Ryan, looked up from his desk when I entered. "Moving out?"

Like Mary's smile, his tone was light. He probably didn't know. "I got laid off. So, yeah."

He spun around. "Seriously?" He paused like I was going to tell him that I was joking. "Kendall, I'm sorry."

The way his voice softened encouraged my tears. I hadn't liked this job. It was okay, but nothing I was passionate about. Selling items like tomato juice and paper cups wasn't what most kids dreamed of. But my coworkers had been cool. Ryan was mellow and an all-around nice guy. All he wanted was to do his job and go home to his family. On the bright side, I'm glad he wasn't fired.

"What are you going to do?" he asked.

That question was on replay in my head. "Find a new job?"

He gave me a steady look that suggested he was thinking what I was thinking. Where the hell was I going to find a marketing gig, and how long would it take? If Mr. Golding laid off a couple more people, they'd be applying for the same positions. And I was a little raw about being released because of my apparent lack of education. I had experience, but not much else that made me stand out past other candidates.

Ryan rubbed a hand over his face. He wheeled out to the edge of the cubicle and looked down the narrow walkway. If anyone had heard my announcement, they were keeping their heads down. Probably afraid they were next on the chopping block.

He scooted back toward his desk. "My sister just quit this job. Maybe you want to try for it?"

My ears perked up. I'd take what prospects I could get.

"I can't really tell you much," he continued. "She had to sign a non-disclosure. But I can tell you that it paid a lot. Like, a lot."

Sounded too good to be true. "But I thought you said she just quit?"

Ryan shrugged. His expression said beggars couldn't be choosers, and I was being too choosy. "Like I said, she couldn't tell me much, and she was pretty frustrated about the whole deal, but it paid a lot."

The *it paid a lot* detail was the clincher. "With what company?"

"I think she might've been asked to move out of state, but I thought she said she applied for it with King Oil. Send me an email and I'll get the info."

Frowning, I sifted through my mind for all the details I could come up with on King Oil. I'd seen their branding enough to know that they were an oil company, locally owned, and out of my league. But they had an opening, so I had a starting point. "Thanks for the heads-up. And thanks for not being a creepy cubicle mate."

"Same to you. I'm still convinced the guy before you stole my lunch at least once a week."

Packing up my desk was as painful as I'd imagined it would be, but it only lasted three minutes. I'd been with the company for close to seven years but had never settled in. Was it any surprise I was the first one let go?

I only needed one of the boxes. Leaving the other one on the desk for the next poor soul that got canned, I swung my winter coat on.

Ryan gave me a solemn nod. "Take care of yourself."

As I walked out of the office, I tried not to look in the other cubicles. I'd be greeted by people who still had their jobs, looking at me like I was walking to the finale of my death sentence.

Anyone I passed on my way out the door cast a confused glance at my box, but then they saw my somber expression and figured out the rest. I stepped out into the cloudy late-winter day. It fit my mood.

I dumped my box in the back seat of my car and slid in behind the wheel. I needed a plan.

I was going to go home and dig out the lease papers. Then the papers and I would wait for Darren to wake up for work.

He'd sign them. He had to. I couldn't afford to move now,

and if I had to move back in with my parents, Darren's gloating would be intolerable.

I parked in front of the cute little house we rented in a historic neighborhood in downtown Billings. For the five years of our marriage, we lived here and I'd made it my home. My siblings had come over to play when they were younger and even slept over—until Darren bitched that it happened too often, or interfered with his sleep, or some other reason he used to distance me from my family.

I parked on the street because Darren insisted on having the garage, claiming I left during daylight hours and didn't suffer the Billings winter like he did. Never mind that his vehicle had remote start and mine didn't.

I could weather one more year, find a new job, and save up.

The house was quiet, but awareness skated over my spine. Was Darren awake already?

Giggles filtered through the house. Ugh. He had a woman over. I didn't care if he dated. At first, it hurt that he'd waited all of three days after we agreed that our marriage was over, but I was determined to move on.

Earlier this year, I'd even had a somewhat steady boyfriend. Until I heard the same tired arguments parroted from him that Darren had used. *Do they have to call all the time? Why can't your parents do more? You don't have to help them.*

I laid my purse and keys on the Italian tile countertop. I was on my way through the kitchen to my bedroom when my gaze landed on the table. There was an unfamiliar backpack sitting on the top with papers spread out next to it.

The lease.

Relief swept through me when I noticed they were signed. Until my gaze landed on the second signature under Darren's, the one that was very much *not* mine.

I fisted them in my hand and stomped in the other direction to Darren's room. Breathy laughs and sultry moans grew louder. I raised my hand to pound on the door, but the door was cracked. I pushed it open instead. My face screwed up at the sight that was now burned into my retinas— Darren's ass swiveling in a not-as-sexy-as-he-hoped striptease.

I shook the papers in my hand. "Want to explain these?"

He whipped around. I'd seen all of him already. Nice body. Decent package that he sort of knew how to use. The woman shrieked and dove behind him. I didn't see much of her, but the glimpse I got was of someone several years younger than me with bottle platinum hair and less padded hips than mine.

I swept my gaze around the room. A Montana State sweater was on the floor at Darren's feet. Did that belong to the backpack owner too? If he was dipping into the college girl pool while pushing thirty, that was his business. All I cared about was the second signature on the lease.

"Fuck, Kendall." Darren didn't bother to cover himself and his flagging erection. He planted his hands on his hips. "What the hell. Knock, will ya?"

This time I wasn't going to be distracted from the real issue. I'd let him do that to me through our marriage and the divorce. "The lease papers are signed, but not by me."

He had the grace to look abashed, and even covered his privates. The news must really be bad. "I was going to talk to you about that tonight."

"Talk now."

The girl cowered behind him, snaking a hand out to grab her sweater.

He cleared his throat. "I'm... Um... This is Daria. We've been seeing each other, and we'd like to move in together."

I reared back like he slapped me. "And you decided this

the week before our lease is up, and figured that this place is as good as any." Because he wouldn't have to do the work of moving.

Just like before. *We're both paying bills. Why don't we live together? Like roommates.*

Why hadn't I taken into consideration what a user Darren was? Divorce hadn't changed him, and I'd been naïve to think otherwise. He might cover his rent, but he ate my groceries and streamed shows off my account. And he was still inept at running a vacuum cleaner.

"Look, Kendall…"

I folded my arms, crinkling the papers, and tapped my foot.

He squared his shoulders, his eyes infusing with determination. He never did like when I stood up to him. "Kendall, I helped you out after the divorce, but you gotta move on."

"You *did not* help me out," I hissed. "We agreed that living together was financially beneficial for both of us. I thought it was understood that the other party would give advanced warning if they wanted the situation to change."

"Well, the situation's changed. Here's your warning."

I wanted to scream. "Your girlfriend needing a place to stay because she's getting kicked out of her sorority doesn't justify less than a week's notice."

The way his eyes flared told me more than I needed to know. I'd guessed the story. I'm sure he was present when she violated whatever rule removed her.

His face hardened into the mulish pout I knew so well. "Daria's moving in, and you need to move out. It's done."

"I hope she gets enough financial aid to keep you solvent in the beer and porn you love so much."

"I wouldn't have needed porn if—"

"Don't you fucking *dare*." Wanting more satisfaction between the sheets didn't mean I was the one lacking. I peered around him to his girlfriend. "I hope you don't have anyone or anything in your life that'll take attention away from him, or he'll make you feel like shit for it. He's immature like that."

"Get out," he roared.

I flung the papers in his face, and they fluttered to the floor. "Gladly. I'm going to find some boxes to pack my shit."

As I was leaving, he took the parting shot. "Have fun moving back in with your parents."

I slammed out of the house and went back to my car. I had no plan of where to go, so I drove aimlessly until I came across a fast food place and pulled in. Not to waste money on food, but I had to come up with a plan of what to do without using more gas.

First of all, I needed a place to live. I spent the next hour calling around, writing down availability dates and amounts. Between the deposit and rent and when I could actually move in, it wasn't looking good.

My phone buzzed. Crap, I forgot to call my youngest brother back. I pulled to the side of the road and answered. "Hey. What's up?"

Wendell's seventh-grade puberty-stricken voice half squeaked, half growled into the phone. "Mom forgot to leave me money for the field trip."

I should've taken his call when I still had my job. This was like a double whammy. "How much do you need?"

"Twenty dollars. And a sack lunch."

"When do you need it?"

"An hour ago." He sniffled. "They took off already. I'm in the library."

My heart cracked for him. "But you only called twenty minutes ago."

"I was trying Mom, but she didn't answer. I thought maybe I could still meet them...that you could drive me..."

"Ah, Wendell. I'm sorry. Is Lenny with you?" They were twins, but Wendall was the youngest in every sense of the word.

"Yeah. We have to sit in the library until school's done."

"Okay." If I ignored my pride and moved back home, I could help Wendell and Lenny out. And my youngest sister that still lived at home. Mom and Dad would happily let me pick up open shifts at the diner and the thrift store. I stared at the people wandering in and out of the restaurant, oblivious to how I was reverting from professional career woman back to my sixteen-year-old self. "I'll swing by and sign you two out and get you to the field trip."

His immense relief was worth it. I never regretted helping my family. Could they rely on me less? Yes. But I was still that little girl watching her mom break down in postpartum depression and roam listlessly through the house. As the oldest, I witnessed her struggle to return to someone who didn't hide in the bathroom and cry.

Didn't mean I wanted to stay living at home. I couldn't help myself or them if I didn't get my loans paid down.

The job Ryan mentioned came to mind. *It paid a lot.* I pulled up his email. I had a mysterious job to apply for.

CHAPTER 2

 entry

BRANDY BURNED its way down my throat. The woman in the slinky red dress sitting on the other side of the bar eyed me with her artfully applied smokey eye.

Only a few months ago, I'd already know her name and be loading her in an elevator, leaning in close, murmuring about how beautiful she was and how sexy she made that dress look, and I'd be thinking of all the wicked things I'd be doing to her.

And then after I carried out each and every thought—in her hotel room, not in my room, house, or cabin because I'd learned my lesson—I'd grab my shoes and sneak out. If I happened to sleep over, I'd wake up for another round on the bed or in the shower or over the bathroom sink, and then I'd leave. I'd run home, take a quick shower, put on a fresh suit, and get to work.

If I didn't sleep over, I'd still wake early and go for a run and then grab a good ol' country breakfast before work.

Setting my glass down, I avoided looking in the direction of the woman. Nothing against her. It was all me.

Rodrigo appeared in front of me. He was wearing a white shirt with black trousers and suspenders, but it was his black mustache that capped the old-time saloon-owner look. He was the reason I loved this bar. Not only was he the bartender, he was the owner and could talk business like a master. This was one of his five bars and restaurants, but it was the only one he worked at.

"Want another?" he asked.

"Nah. I've gotta drive home."

He appraised me. He'd never asked what was different, but by the way he studied me, he'd noticed that I was done with women. "The lady in red has been asking about you."

I took another sip, ending up taking a bigger drink than usual, and hissed through the familiar burn. "What'd you say?"

"I said that you'd be stupid not to be interested, but that you come here to think about work, not play." He tipped his head toward me. "I didn't tell her that you're Gentry King."

"Accurate, and thank you." It didn't take more than a few minutes of talking to Rodrigo all those years ago to know that he succeeded in business because he could read people. He also knew how I'd used my name and the oil empire I ran to get enough women in my day. Which wasn't that long ago.

He wiped down the bar around me. "You wouldn't have thanked me six months ago."

"Nope." I wasn't going to tell him why. If I sounded callous and superficial in my head, what would it be like to voice the reason why I quit messing around? "My son got married last fall."

"I remember when you told me he was engaged. Congrats, man."

I slid my elbows on the counter, hands folded in front of me, and sighed. I never talked about my kids' business with anyone.

He peered at me. "Not a reason for congratulations?"

"It should be. His new wife is a nice girl. Sweet. Montana born and raised."

"But?"

I needed to quit talking. "I don't know if he loves her."

Rodrigo cocked his head. "Then why marry?"

Wasn't that the hundred-million-dollar question that only a few knew the answer to. "Aiden was under pressure to get married."

"I know that wasn't from you."

And it wasn't from Aiden's mother. Everyone knew my story. *King Oil CEO loses wife in tragic accident.*

It was no fucking accident. Manslaughter was what the meth-head who beat my wife to death got. I called it murder, but the courts hadn't agreed. And by the time they passed their sentence on the perpetrator, I was steeping myself in so much sex that I didn't have to think about how unfair it was that I was left alone to raise four boys and run a company that wasn't my family's legacy. Well, it wasn't before I met Sarah. Once she died, it'd been my sole purpose to keep it running at full potential and secure my four boys' fortune.

Then I learned what Sarah did with that fortune.

"My wife," I finally answered, even though it wasn't an answer. "She…before she died…" Business was too ingrained in me. I couldn't tell Rodrigo the story behind the marriage. It was family business, and Sarah's mother would go nuclear if she learned I said anything. I said something parallel with the truth.

"My wife's mother is determined to see all the kids married." Happily or not.

Confusion crinkled Rodrigo's brow. "So, your son got married to please his grandmother?"

"Basically." There was nothing grandmotherly about Emilia Boyd.

"Hmm." He was smart enough to know there was a crap ton I wasn't saying. Like how my late wife Sarah got the payout of her parents' partial sale of the oil company and tied it up in a trust for each of our four boys. A trust that played too fast and hard with their future by setting a deadline for when they should get married.

I'd raised them to work hard and take care of themselves. Fuck their trust money. But their grandmother had a much different opinion about losing the money, a somewhat legitimate reason. And she was a force on a good day. The result had me at the graveside, asking, "What the hell, Sarah?" more times than I could count.

I wasn't good company, even for myself, tonight. I knocked on the countertop and rose. "I'd better head home."

"Gentry." Rodrigo didn't shout my name. Billings, Montana, was small enough that even if people didn't recognize King Oil's CEO in person, they'd know my uncommon first name. "Aiden's a good kid. A good man. He'll take care of his wife."

My smile was small. "She won't go without, that's for sure." Unless it was love, laughter, and a warm, inviting home. Then she was on her own.

As I walked to my pickup, I couldn't help but replay my argument with Aiden the night before his wedding, which had conveniently been two days before his twenty-ninth birthday, the day the rules of his trust would kick in.

It's just money, Aiden. Don't start your marriage with a lie.

My marriage, my business. He'd shot me a stubborn look that was so similar to his mother's. *My* money, *my business.*

You let your Grams make it her business. Sarah's father passed away years ago, but her mother, Emilia, owned controlling shares of King Oil. And as soon as she'd learned about the trust situation, she'd badgered Aiden about getting married.

Not even Grams can force me to marry. Kate's a nice girl. What are you complaining about?

Exactly. She's a nice girl. How do you think she'll feel to know you're not with her because you love her?

Aiden's hard features had turned even stonier. *Women are a means to help us get what we want. Isn't that what you've always taught us?*

I loved your mother, and when she died—

Did you? Or was it because you walked right into a multi-million-dollar job and marriage once she got pregnant? Because you sure jumped into her best friend's bed quick enough after she died. Aiden had stepped into my space, his normally rigid countenance filled with anger, startling me. It'd been a long time since I'd seen any emotion in him. *And everyone else's bed. Women got you through the grief. Women got you through your mid-life crisis; women get you through the stress of your job. So, Kate is going to help me get what I want, and if you don't want to see her hurt, then don't tell her.*

He'd stormed away, and my past unloaded on me. Fifteen years of indiscreetly sleeping around, and I saw in one instant how my kids judged my actions and were paying it forward in a harsh way. Not only that, but if Aiden's attitude was an indicator, none of them thought very highly of me.

They thought me sleeping around so soon after their mother's death meant I hadn't cared about her. They knew that we didn't get engaged because we'd been crazy in love. She got pregnant when we were eighteen, and I'd married her as soon as we got our diplomas—thanks to pressure from her parents. But I had loved her though. Losing her gutted me. I hadn't wanted to raise our kids without her. She'd been my partner and my best friend.

I hadn't found anyone else I was willing to partner with like her. But ours hadn't been a sweeping, romantic love story. We'd been young and willing to stick it out for the sake of our kid. Then another kid. And another. And another. We got caught up in the whole family thing, figured we might as well get the child-bearing years out of the way so we could have our fun when we were older.

Our parents helped us, but when hers had offered me a position at the oil company, I'd jumped on it. Sarah had run my family ranch that was now my youngest son's career.

I slid into my pickup and shut the door behind me. There was an unmistakable bite in the air, and the news was forecasting snow. I had a work trip in the morning, but I should make it to Wyoming and back before the weather got too bad.

Honestly, it wouldn't matter if I was in Wyoming or my house. It'd be me and an empty room. I was getting used to spending my nights alone. My heavy travel schedule required a lot of hotel stays that had come with plenty of opportunities to meet new women. Learning to live with myself was a good thing.

If I kept telling myself that, I might believe that I didn't miss the married life as much as I thought.

My phone rang, saving me from my thoughts. I answered using the control on the steering wheel.

Emilia's voice blazed through the cab. My stomach clenched—my usual stress response when it came to her. Good thing I stuck with one drink.

"Gentry."

That was her hello. Saying your name like it was a curse

word. Sarah had been the best of both her parents, missing Emilia's thorny personality and no-BS attitude and her dad's business acumen, which had been dubious at best.

"Emilia, what can I do for you?" Call me an ass-kisser, but this woman still held my job in her hands. She owned controlling shares of King Oil, and I think she'd want to be buried with the paperwork in her cold dead hands. Oil had been discovered on land she and DB no longer owned but had held mineral rights to. The fight over that with the landowners had been contentious, but in the end, Emilia and Boyd came out on top.

They'd built the exploration and production company, becoming one of the most successful E&Ps in the continental US. After DB died, Emilia sold some leaseholds and promoted me to CEO. She'd also changed the name to King Oil. Which had surprised me, but with Emilia, there was always a reason, and it was to brand the company with my family's Montana legacy. Between DB and the original landowners and our neighbors, the Cartwrights, the company needed a fresh image. It was probably why they'd pushed Sarah and me to marry.

"I need the jet," Emilia barked. "I have a job applicant I need to fly to Denver."

What the hell was in Denver? I knew what was there for me. My second son, Beckett. He owned a tech company that he ran out of Denver, but he used the company's Learjet as often as I did. But I knew visiting Beckett wasn't the reason Emilia was interested in Denver. She'd never been an involved grandparent unless it was to teach the kids about investor shares and fracking.

"I'm taking it for a meeting in Wyoming tomorrow. You'll have to talk to the pilots, but it might be free after that."

"She can go with you."

"Who?" In Emilia's mind, the jet was King Oil property

and, therefore, hers. Never mind that Aiden and I used it often for work, as did Beck. Xander wandered the world, but hardly touched our private plane. And Dawson didn't leave the ranch.

"Her name is Kendall Brinkley, and she needs to get to Denver to interview with Beck."

"With Beckett?" What the hell was she doing hiring people for Beck? He bought and sold apps and programs. If it wasn't black gold, Emilia didn't have time for it. And she resented that Beckett had gone into business himself and didn't lend his talents to the company.

"Wilma quit," she said as if that answered everything.

Beckett's long-time grandmotherly assistant had left to move to Florida. That didn't answer what Emilia was doing hiring his assistants, but fighting her was a losing battle. "All right. Give Ms. Brinkley instructions to the Billings airport and let her know to be there at nine. The Wyoming stop is first, and she needs to be comfortable flying to Colorado herself."

"She'll be fine." I thought she was done with me, but no. "And Gentry."

"Yes, Emilia."

Her voice sparked like a cattle prod. "Keep your hands off this one. I mean it."

CHAPTER 3

 endall

A PRIVATE PLANE. I wasn't bolstered by the fact that Ms. Boyd didn't answer my leading questions about if this was really an escort gig. The job sounded like the real deal, even if I did interview at a restaurant I could never afford to eat at and not at King Oil headquarters. But then I could be flying off to get trafficked, and my family would know nothing about it thanks to all the contracts I signed.

That's a non-disclosure. It means if you talk about any of this, or anything related to this job or my family, I will sue you. And I will win. I don't pay obscene amounts of retainer fees to employ rookies.

Emilia Boyd scared the shit out of me. But through her hard demeanor, not once did she call me honey, dear, or sweetie like so many of my older clients had. She didn't dumb down what she was saying. If she felt like she had to explain something, she laid out a description and moved on.

I felt more respected for my brain in the twenty minutes I spent with her than I had at any point in my other career.

Last night, I'd spent hours researching Beckett King online. Tech savvy. Owned his own company. Made more in a year than I'll make in a lifetime. What startled me the most was that he was a King, but didn't work for King Oil. Yet, Ms. Boyd had interviewed me for his executive assistant opening.

I also couldn't figure out why the company was named after Beckett's dad's side and not the Boyds. But I'd stumbled across an article about the sale and rebranding. Smart move. Donald "DB" Boyd had fueled a gossip mill in Montana for being just shy of a crook. It had hurt the company's reputation nationally and threatened to spill over the growth the company planned internationally. And if uncompromising Ms. Boyd would be considered a bitch by today's misogynistic standards, then fifty years ago, she probably landed on several corporate shit lists.

She'd called me last night and told me I'd be flying out today with Gentry King. Holy ballsacks, as my oldest brother, Brendell, would say.

Gentry King.

I'd spent more time than I should searching for everything I could find on him. If I was going to get sold off, I should at least know who was making the sale. Turned out, he was more likely to eat me alive than sell me.

A shiver traced down my spine. Several articles pegged him at close to forty-nine.

Gentry King did not look like he was in his late forties. In the pictures, he was usually with a drop-dead gorgeous woman at his side that likely didn't grow up eating Dinty Moore beef stew and canned peas while her parents worked late. His eyes crinkled at the corners, but there wasn't a single wrinkle on his face. The maturity that lined his features kept my gaze lingering longer and longer on each photo. But that's what happened when I'd been married to a man-child who thought I should still do his laundry after our divorce.

Mr. King was almost twenty years older than me. I could find him attractive, but I had no business lusting after him if we were sharing a plane ride.

Ms. Boyd's words ran through my mind. *Don't worry about the interview with Beck. He's got a good heart, and I'm his grandmother. He'll give you the job. But I want you to call me. Nailing the interview is the first phase.*

First phase of what? I had asked.

We'll talk when we reach that point.

What the hell was going on?

I gripped the handle on the door and gave my car one last look. Should I leave a note for my parents in case I didn't come back? All I told them was that I was flying to Denver for an interview, and they wished me luck—and asked if I'd be home to pick up the early morning shifts at the diner this weekend.

That was the shove I needed to accept the interview.

I hauled my luggage out. Picking my way over the slippery parking lot, I tucked my chin into my plain brown winter parka and went to the entrance Ms. Boyd described. A freaking private plane.

My luggage wheeled behind me. The squeaky wheel echoed into the morning with my heel strikes. I wish I could've worn my leggings and a sweater for the trip, but I had little idea about when and where the interview would take place. Ms. Boyd just said there'd be a driver waiting for me in Denver.

Warmth flowed over me as I stepped inside. I continued to the waiting room I was instructed to take a seat in, but as soon as I stepped off the entry carpet, my heel slid out from under me.

I squeezed my eyes shut, but a "Fuck!" escaped because wouldn't that be my luck? I was going to tumble across the private jet lounge in a skirt and heels, getting nice and gritty.

My landing never happened. Strong arms latched around me and centered me back on my feet. "There you go."

My rescuer's scent wrapped around me like a warm blanket. That deep rumble of his could fuel a gal's wicked dreams. And I'd just shouted a curse word that I'm sure the whole building heard.

Turning around, I attempted to straighten my coat and tug my skirt back down. "Oh, thank you, I'm sorry about swearing—" My gaze landed on my rescuer. It was him. King Oil's CEO and the dad of the man I was supposed to get an interview with. "Mr. King."

He gave me that half-smile he always had in the pictures and looked me over. "You didn't hurt yourself, did you?" His brow furrowed as he looked at my skirt. It was maroon and knee-length. My heels were from boots that nearly reached my knees. I wasn't going to wander around in the middle of winter in completely bare legs.

I used the moment to study him. He was real. Not a picture on a screen. The threads of silver at his temples did nothing to detract from his vitality. It was like he only allowed gray hairs where they enhanced his handsome, chiseled face.

"No. I'm fine." And apparently breathless. "Thank you again."

His gaze lifted to my face, and he looked like he'd sucked a lemon wedge out of his iced tea. "You're not with the flight crew, are you."

It wasn't a question. Was that a bad thing? I stuck my hand out. "Kendall Brinkley."

He studied me. Slowly, he clasped my hand, hot, roughened skin sliding over mine.

My body wanted to melt into the strength and heat coming off him. He was a hundred times more potent than anything Darren put out.

He abruptly released my hand and stuffed it into his pants pockets, his mouth turned down like he was pained. He wore a charcoal suit. He wore the hell out of the suit, and I'm sure it was a Tom Ford or something along those lines. I doubted we shopped in the same atmospheric layer. Hell, I doubted he did any of his own shopping.

"Have a seat, Ms. Brinkley. I'll check with the flight crew about when we can board." He disappeared into a side room that he must've popped out of in time to save me.

The sense of dismissal left a wake of hurt. Ridiculous. I needed a job, not a boyfriend. I needed a job more than I needed hot, sweaty sex—and I liked hot, sweaty sex a lot. I bet that's how it was with Mr. King.

I gripped my battered and frayed black suitcase and went into the empty lounge, choosing a seat in the corner where I could lick my wounds. As if I'd ever be in the league of Gentry King. Or any of his four shockingly gorgeous and stupidly rich sons.

I'd read all the tabloids, and it wasn't just local media that hunted Mr. King. He'd been featured all over the world, and not just for his successful business. He was at openings of restaurants in Paris, at a play on Broadway, and standing under the bright sun in Qatar. Always with a woman on his arm.

There wasn't much about him from before his wife died, but there was a lot after. Seeing him in person didn't diminish my attraction. It was the dichotomy. Compared to my ex-husband, Gentry was another species. Compared to *me*, he was another species.

But a play on Broadway? That'd be fun.

I sighed and crossed my legs, staring out the large picture

window where a jet was parked. I guess there were worse things than working for a King.

Mr. King emerged from the room with a young woman dressed in a pilot's uniform. She wore a wedding ring—not that I checked—and was talking in a brusque tone.

"I can get you to Douglas, Mr. King. But going on to Denver may be a problem."

Mr. King's brows dropped, and he looked toward me. I was about to hastily look away, to not be caught staring, but his eyes were like tracking beacons. A dark brown that caught the lights and pierced deep into my soul. Only, his jaw clenched like I was the last person he wanted to drag onto the plane.

He dragged his gaze back to the pilot. "The meeting in Douglas is paramount. If you think we can beat the weather, let's do it. We'll figure Denver out later."

Dread shot through me. I might get stranded in Wyoming? If I could get per diem and room and board off Ms. Boyd for a few extra days, I wasn't turning it down. But if I could get to Denver and secure a job with this family, I'd rather do that. How many applicants were vying for the position while we were detouring to Wyoming?

The pilot disappeared. Mr. King, hands in pockets, strolled to the window and stared out of it. He didn't look at me when he spoke. "Would getting stranded in Wyoming be a problem for you?"

Yes. "No, Mr. King."

That got him to turn his head, a dark brow lifted. "Would you miss work? A family?"

"No, on both accounts." I wasn't about to tell a guy that worked for one of the wealthiest oil companies in the country, who had ranched sweeping acres while he ran that company, and raised four boys by himself that I was unemployed and single and had no major accomplishments to my name at twenty-eight years old.

"Did you quit your job when you interviewed with Emilia?"

"No. I'm between jobs."

The eyebrow kicked back up.

Nerves made me chatter. I didn't want to ramble around Mr. King, but I wasn't born to play it as cool as him. "I was let go. Downsizing. I only have a four-year degree, not a masters, so I was the first to go."

He did a half-turn away from the window. "What'd you do for work?"

"I was in marketing."

"Weren't you good at your job?"

What the hell? I clutched the handle of my suitcase. "Yes. I was really good. And I made the company a lot of money. But he felt that someone who is more educated has the potential to make more money."

He slowly shook his head. "Then your boss is a schmuck." He turned back to the window. The conversation was done, but I was left fighting a small smile.

Mr. Golding *was* a schmuck, and his bottom-line would prove it.

Mr. King lifted his chin like he was signaling someone. I peered out the window. The plane's door was open, and a woman was flagging us down.

He stepped toward me and beckoned toward my suitcase. "May I?"

My mind froze. He was close, and his fresh soapy smell and woodsy cologne surrounded me. "May you what?" I rose.

That earned the hint of a smile. "Take your suitcase." He was a good five inches taller than me. Without my heels, he'd be more like seven inches taller. I'd fit perfectly tucked into his side.

"I-I can get it."

He bent and wrapped his big hand around the handle. "Allow me."

"Okay." Did I need an advanced degree to talk to Mr. King? I had to quit letting him affect me. I wasn't one to live in fantasy worlds.

He opened the door and ushered me out. The entire walk to the plane, he was right next to me, his hand held out behind me like he was ready to play catch with my falling ass. But he didn't touch me.

I scurried up the steps and into the chill of the jet. It was hard not to stop at the entry and stare. I stumbled toward the plush seats, looking around. Varnished wood trim. Leather seats. And a room with a door open that looked like a bedroom.

I was on a plane with a bedroom with the King Oil CEO. I...didn't hate being in this situation.

The flight attendant closed the door, blocking the chill, and took my luggage from Mr. King. His had probably been loaded before he'd caught me in his strong arms. How early had he gotten to the airport? He probably did more before five a.m. than I did all day.

I selected a chair toward the middle. Mr. King conversed quietly with the crew and chose a seat up front. Disappointment snaked through me. Why did I think he would be bothered to sit by me? I was supposed to impress his son, not him.

The flight attendant approached, wearing a genuine smile. "Hi, Ms. Brinkley. I'm Shirley, and I'm happy to be flying with you to Douglas."

I returned her friendly smile. "How long will the flight be?"

"About an hour and a half. Then I understand that if the weather allows, you'll continue with us to Denver. Would you like a blanket or pillow? Water? Soda? I'll bring out the snacks after we're in the air."

"A blanket, please." If the weather allows. As long as I wasn't stranded in Middle of Nowhere, Wyoming, I was fine. I needed that job, and this trip was wasting a lot of quality job-hunting time.

The flight was smooth and quiet. When the plane bumped down for a landing, I peered outside, dismayed to see snow steadily falling. Gusts of wind picked up piles, swirling flakes in the air.

Once Shirley gave us the go-ahead to unbuckle, she murmured to Mr. King. His expression darkened, and he glanced at the cockpit, then nodded.

The pilot emerged, her face grim. They spoke in low tones, and I eased my way forward. Shirley retrieved my ragged suitcase from a storage bin I hadn't seen before.

"There's no helping it." Mr. King spoke to Shirley. "Do you have a place to stay?"

Shirley spoke. "My aunt lives in Converse County, not far away from Douglas. She's on her way to get both of us."

"Good. I'll find a hotel for Ms. Brinkley and I after the meeting. Have a safe trip, and let me know when you settle." He exhaled and seemed reluctant to turn toward me, when he did his gaze was direct and his expression heavy, like he was delivering bad news. "It looks like we're snowed in at Douglas after all."

entry

THE DRIVER HAD A RED SUV—AN all-wheel drive, thank God —all warmed up, the windows defrosted, and he was parked as close to the plane as he was allowed. I waved the flight crew off my carry-on as I hit the bottom of the steps out of the plane. Snow whipped around us, the wind howling around buildings and over jets. I turned and took the suitcase from Ms. Brinkley. She blinked in surprise but was too distracted picking her way across the snow-covered stairs to argue.

She gingerly stepped on the pavement. Those boots of hers were going to be little more than cold ice skates. No matter how long and curvy they made her legs look, they were useless. I'd offer my arm, but my hands were full. Instead, I ushered her to the waiting car. The driver helped load our items.

Ms. Brinkley slipped into the warm car. The wind was likely heading straight up that skirt.

I usually sat in the back. I was able to chat with the driver but could take a call without talking right into his ear. But I'd started avoiding Ms. Brinkley as soon as her solid weight landed in my arms. That was bad enough, but when she turned those luminous teal eyes my way, I knew I had to keep my distance. Too many inconvenient questions came to mind when I looked at her.

Was she single? Was she going to interview with Beckett to seduce him? Was she into older men?

It was ridiculous. The female company I usually kept was closer to my own age, maybe dipping as low as their early thirties. Still older than my kids. Older than all my kids. I doubted Kendall Brinkley was older than Aiden.

I climbed into the front seat. Ethan gave me a smile, already chatting with Ms. Brinkley. He insisted I use his first name long ago, saying Mr. Keplin was his dad.

"Where are you parked, Ethan?" I asked.

He started the car, the tires crunching in the rapidly piling snow. "In the employee lot."

"How about we drive around there." I adjusted my suit coat. My heavier jacket was rolled into my carry-on bag, and I wish I had the insulated boots I wore on the ranch.

"Sir?"

"You're going home. I'm still paying you, but I want you to settle in before this gets too bad."

"Oh, no, sir—"

I cut him off with a look. He wanted to do his job. But the guy had a wife and three little girls. There was no way I was tying him up in this weather. He did as I asked, thanking me profusely. I rushed around to the driver's side of the SUV and got in. Adjusting the rearview mirror, I could see Ms. Brinkley peering up into the front and then out the window.

"Looks like I'm your driver today." I pulled out of the airport and onto the roads where traffic was going at a snail's pace. I already knew what would happen when I reached the meeting place. Our time would be cut as short as possible. But I was the last to arrive, and we had reports to discuss that had to be done in person. All the players were in town for this meeting, and I had to fire the people doctoring the site inspection reports.

The rest of the drive took my concentration as I focused on where the road should be. A white blanket covered the expanse of pavement. The wind wasn't strong enough to blow it all off. I followed barely visible tracks that had been left by vehicles that hopefully had the good sense to get off the road.

As I pulled up to our Douglas headquarters, I did what I'd been trying to avoid and looked at Ms. Brinkley. It was the middle of the day, but the thick clouds and heavy snow made it feel like evening. She was squinting out the window at the square two-story building, her elegant profile making it hard to put my eyes back on the road.

Parking as close to the door as possible, I glared at the building. I'd been against purchasing this well-drilling company. I'm all for helping the little guy, but these guys never seemed to want to help themselves, and I had suspected safety wasn't a priority. Emilia had forced the issue. I couldn't wait for the day she retired, but I was starting to suspect that I'd be retiring earlier.

"You might as well come inside, Ms. Brinkley." I gathered my case and looked over my shoulder. Her soft scent filled the space. It was too pleasing. Not quite flowery, but just shy of perfumey. "The way this snow is building and how sticky it is, I don't want it building up around the muffler and suffocating you."

That would take hours and a ton of snow. I just didn't want her sitting out here alone.

She cocked a brow full of attitude, but smoothed it over so quickly I thought I was imagining it. "Okay."

"What?"

"Hmm?" Her brow puckered in such a dainty way I wanted to smooth it over. Strands of her hair stuck out from the tight roll in the back of her head. She looked slightly disheveled, and it was cute as hell.

"You didn't like my suggestion."

"No, it's fine. I'm okay going inside."

"But?" I wasn't leaving until I learned what I said wrong. Most people who weren't family acted a certain way around me. She hadn't been around me enough to school her reaction, and I enjoyed seeing more than professional acquiescence. I enjoyed seeing real emotion caused by me on her face even if it was irritation.

"Well, I mean, I was born and raised in Montana. I think I know what to do in a vehicle in a snow storm."

She struck me into silence for a couple of heartbeats. A chuckle bubbled out of me. "All right then. What would you like to do?"

She sucked the corner of her bottom lip in, her shoulders hunched like she was sheepish. "I'd like to come in."

My laughter grew stronger. "So, you're not irritated because I ordered you around but because I unintentionally questioned your intelligence?"

"I'm a peon. I'm used to being ordered around."

My humor faded as my mind went south and I pictured her on her knees, looking up at me with those expressive eyes. *I'm used to being ordered around.* I turned around and got out, letting the cold wind slap some sense into me. Before I could open her door, she was out. I left the car running but locked the doors.

She was tucked into the brown parka that looked like it could be mistaken for a mud bog and stuffed her hands in her pockets. More strands of her hair buffeted around her head. I held my elbow out for two reasons. One, those boots of hers. Two, because I'd been raised with manners—not because I wanted to feel her against me again. She eyed my arm like it was a rattler shaking its tail, but she tucked her hand into the crook of my elbow. Her grip was sturdy and practical, like the rest of her.

On the way to the door, I said, "You might wish you stayed in the vehicle, Ms. Brinkley."

THE MEETING WAS as tense and dramatic as I thought it'd be. The board that ran the drilling company "had no idea" what I was talking about, as if Aiden and I hadn't hired expert field techs to tell us exactly what was going on. The managers wouldn't listen to the supervisors about what was failing at the local wells, and someone was going to get hurt or killed.

Well, they had to listen to me, which meant it was too late.

Ms. Brinkley damn near ran from the meeting once I dismissed it, and I wasn't far behind. My reason for rushing was the weather. Hers was likely to escape the massive awkwardness. I should've had her wait outside, but the way she affected me was…concerning. I let the others assume she was an assistant and thought that seeing me mass fire employees would sour my image in her eyes—if she was the type to go after older men.

As soon as she was settled in the front seat, I pulled away from the headquarters and plowed through the growing drifts into the parking lot and onto the road. The wind was stronger, and the snow was lighter, lowering visibility in town. Outside of city limits, the roads were probably impossible to navigate.

A blue and white sign for a hotel chain came into view. I pulled in under the canopy.

"Want to come inside this time?"

Her wide eyes slid toward me, then back to the dash. "No, thank you."

She was a Montana girl born and bred. It wasn't the weather spooking her. "Ms. Brinkley."

"Yes." She didn't look at me.

"Do I have to keep asking what's on your mind, or are you going to tell me?"

Her shoulders eased and she turned more in her seat. "That was intense."

"Firing an entire team? Yes." My plan might've paid off, but it left me with a sour taste. I didn't want her to fear me, and I shouldn't care what she thought.

"You can really shut them out of everything remotely?" Her voice was filled with awe. Huh.

"Yes. We had it scheduled to do at a certain time. Their behavior and inaction was thoroughly documented."

"I heard that part."

"People could get killed on oil wells. People *have* gotten killed." I stared out the passenger window and through the glass doors of the hotel. No one was in the hotel. "I once visited a guy who'd been in an explosion. He'd gotten badly burned and lost part of both legs." I chuffed out a breath. "My lawyer told me not to, but I went anyway. The guy was barely old enough to drink. He was lying in bed, one arm bandaged, the lab girl was trying to get blood from his other arm, and his legs were... They just weren't there. He was angry. So angry at the world. And at me. I couldn't blame him. Ultimately, I'm responsible." I switched my gaze to her, getting lost in her wide stare. "I don't want it to happen again."

"What was his name?"

Why the hell had I told her that? I didn't know more than her name. And that she was in marketing. "Jack."

I got out of the vehicle before I could spill any more details of my life. She didn't follow me.

Inside, I stomped the snow off my boots and went to the counter. A woman politely smiled at me. "I'm so sorry. We're full."

That stopped me in my tracks. "Full?"

"There was a hockey tournament in town, and they're all stranded. Motorists off the highway snatched the rest up."

Her words echoed in my head. Sleeping in my car in the middle of a blizzard wasn't desirable, but I was also responsible for someone else, thanks to Emilia. "Do you know of any place that might have openings?"

"Let me call around and check."

I gave her a grateful smile. "Do you mind? I'm sure it's been a busy night."

She waved it off and picked up the receiver. "We do it for each other all the time. On days like this, you shouldn't be driving all over town."

"I appreciate it."

As she made call after call, I milled around. My options were limited. A twenty-four-hour truck stop might let us park there for the night. We'd have amenities and gas since we'd be continuously running the engine. I doubted we could get back out to the airport and bunk down in the lounge, if it was even open.

Two rooms. That was all we needed.

"Sir?" The clerk had the phone under her chin, the cord dangling. "The Hotel LaBelle has one room open. It's downtown."

One room?

One. Room.

I glanced outside. Snow, snow, and more snow. Did I have any options? It was a roof over our head, warm, and had beds. "I'd better not pass it up. The Hotel LaBelle?" I'd only been downtown a few times, but I could find it. "Thank you."

I left, making a mental note to phone the manager and compliment her effort.

The task coming up was nearly as daunting as the firing had been. Back in the vehicle, Kendall expectantly watched me. I kicked the vehicle into gear. "There's one room open at a hotel downtown."

"One room?" Her voice had gone high. She cleared her throat. "Only one?"

"She called everywhere. It's our only option."

"Oh. Okay."

Yeah. She sounded about how I felt. Shell-shocked and full of dread. I had spent the night with plenty of strangers, but never with a woman I wasn't having sex with. And Ms. Brinkley was off-limits.

There were only a few other cars on the road. Twice, I had to gun it through some sizable drifts until I rolled into a spot in the mostly full parking lot behind the hotel.

I killed the engine, and the cold crept in fast, but neither of us moved.

"I guess I'm not surprised this is the one with a room open," she finally said. The stout brick building in front of us wasn't the oldest building in downtown Douglas, but it was close. It certainly wasn't the largest business in this section of town.

We got out, grabbed our bags, and hurried inside. This time there was no offering to carry her bags or help her across the lot. The snow was past the tops of our feet, and a nice knee-deep drift blocked the door.

I pummeled through the drift and shouldered through the door, holding it open for her. Dim light filled the entry. The cream-colored walls looked dingier under the glow and the frayed carpet nearly as old as the structure.

The main area was moderately better with a sparse check-in counter and two chairs by an end table, a rack of brochures on display. Another table lined the wall across from the counter. The carpet was decidedly cleaner, and the walls had old wallpaper, but it was well-cared for. Good. Maybe the room would actually be comfortable.

An older lady with graying hair tied into two braids running down her back grinned. "Glad you could make it. Come on in. The name's Gale, and I'll get you settled right quick."

"It's a cold one out there," I said, going up to the desk and dropping my bag at my feet.

Ms. Brinkley hung back, clutching her bag like it was a life preserver.

"How many nights will you need it for?"

I was about to say one, but I paused. "How long is this weather supposed to last?"

Gale grimaced. "Gosh, we've already surpassed forecasted snow totals. I think the town will be shut down tomorrow for sure. It'll take a full day after that to get the main roads cleared."

"Can I leave it open-ended?"

"Absolutely. We're rarely booked up solid." She ran my card and gave us a key. A real key, not a key card. "Room 201 is up the stairs. We don't have an official continental breakfast, but I also run the bakery next door. My apartment's in the back, so I usually put out a batch of baked goods in the morning. I'll make a few extra batches since you're all stuck."

Gale pointed us to the stairs, and in only a minute we were standing outside room 201. The click of the key in the lock rang ominous down the otherwise quiet hallway. I opened the door and was greeted by darkness.

Flipping the light switch with one hand, I held the door open with the other. "Ladies first."

Ms. Brinkley's eye roll wasn't as contained as she thought. She trekked in and stopped, her gaze glued to the right. I closed the door behind us, flipped the lock, and looked around.

When my gaze landed on what she saw, only one word came to mind.

"Fuck."

endall

ONE BED. There was only one bed. And it wasn't king-sized.

Was it even queen-sized?

"Okay," Mr. King's deep voice rumbled behind me. "I can sleep on the…"

I desperately looked around the room. The wall was lined with a dresser that had a small flat-screen TV on it and an old desk that was nothing but four legs and two drawers. The only other seating option in the room was the desk chair, which was a level below what Mr. Golding had ordered for us in the office.

"Sorry," Mr. King said. "I didn't mean to swear."

"It's okay, Mr. King. I think the situation calls for it."

He roamed around the bed. The only other space in the room was a three-foot-wide path around the bed. Cozy. The comforter was the most modern thing in the room. Cream with reds and browns, it matched the older maroon thick paneled drapes over the window. The wood grain of the furniture was darker than the deep brown carpet. Everything seemed clean and well-cared for, but dated a good twenty years. Maybe thirty. Except for the comforter and TV.

His gaze lifted. The striking intensity in the depths of his amber eyes carried my internal thermostat higher. "Home sweet home."

For a night. Or two. "Yeah, uh. It's a small room." I circled around, looking for the best spot to put my suitcase. All I owned in the world was pared down inside this ratty luggage.

I found a luggage rack in the closet that had less room than my old refrigerator. Muscling my bag on it, I managed not to grunt. Mr. King set his bag on the desk and unloaded his laptop. As I unzipped my bag, I peeked at him from the corner of my eye. He shrugged off his suit coat and draped it over the chair. His white shirt stretched over broad shoulders, and his muscled chest couldn't be more obvious.

"Make yourself comfortable, Ms. Brinkley. I have work to do."

"Are you hungry?" I was starving. The charcuterie plate on the plane didn't hold me past noon, and we'd had no real lunch. Supper wasn't looking good. "I can go round something up."

A faint smile tipped his lips. "And here I'm the rancher. Sure, whatever you can find."

I doubted that what I found was anything he'd eaten before.

Heading back downstairs, I used the time to myself to have a little panic attack. Alone with Mr. King. One bed. Sleeping next to Mr. King.

Who was I kidding? I wasn't going to get any sleep.

∾

GALE WAS busy wiping off the table. She peered over her shoulder. "Oh, hey. I was just going to raid my pantry for snacks. I figured you're all going to be missing dinner."

"That's so generous of you. I can't imagine any of us expect you to feed the whole hotel."

She squatted and tugged out a bin that was stored underneath. "Over half of my guests are long-term residents. They have the suites and probably their own food, as long as the electricity stays on. That only leaves ten rooms, with mostly single travelers that struck out of getting a room at the bigger chains right off the busy roads."

"Can I help with anything?" Please. I couldn't go back to that room. Mr. King was working. The TV would bother him, and I didn't bring anything to read. Maybe I could sacrifice some data and download a book on my phone.

"You don't need me putting you to work. Might as well enjoy a little relaxation time with your husband."

My laugh was nervous as I felt. "We're not married. We're not…together. It's a business trip. An awkward one."

She paused over her task of riffling through the tub of napkins and paper plates, her eyes twinkling. "The whole one bed bit doesn't help."

"Yep." I tugged at my suit coat. It was a little too form-fitted. Once in my life, I'd like to be able to tailor my clothes. Take a little out at the bust and the hips and find a way to keep material from bunching around my waist. It was like I had to pick between modesty and covering my ass as I bent over to grab a fallen pen.

She eyed me. "You don't want to go back to your room, do ya?"

"Is it that obvious? He seems nice and all, but I literally just met him today. I was supposed to go interview for…a different arm of the company."

Straightening, she chuckled. "That's going to make a good

story someday. Downright scandalous if this snow starts taking down power lines."

My heart clambered into my throat. "I hope not."

"Don't worry. This place has a backup generator. Why don't you get napkins and plates arranged, and I'll go in the back and see what I can find." She tapped the bin with the toe of her loafer. When she left, her lips twitched like she was fighting a grin.

The task Gale gave me didn't last nearly as long as I hoped, but she returned, her arms laden with bowls, bags of bread, and a jar of peanut butter.

"I hope no one's allergic." She unloaded all her items, and I helped her line them up. "I usually have that stuff made from sunflower seeds, but it's my favorite so it's gone."

"I love me some SunButter. Do you mind if I make a couple of sandwiches and bring them up?"

"Help yourself. You get first pick. Make sure to grab some apples for later tonight. I also have a few cases of water I save for emergencies."

"I hate to use up all your emergency stock."

She shrugged and started for the door behind the desk. "I'll fill some jugs just in case we lose water. And I haven't raided the bakery yet."

Once she disappeared, I dug out the bread. Gale had also brought a jar of grape jelly. What would the bakery items be? My stomach rumbled. This was fine dining for me. What would Mr. King think?

I peered outside. Darkness had settled early, thanks to the cloud cover and continuing snow. Now it was falling in steady huge chunks. Every once in a while, the wind would kick a few swirls around by the door, but other than that it was hard to tell how deep it was. Unexpected roomie or not, I was glad to be indoors.

I'd miss my interview. I gasped. Oh no! I hadn't thought

to call Ms. Boyd about the interview. The way Mr. King handled that meeting…

The hunger pangs in my belly turned to flutters. He'd been commanding, firm, and efficient. The three people he'd fired had all tried to argue and he'd shut them down. None of it was an act. He had the reports and data to back up everything he accused them of. They were lucky to only lose their jobs—and he'd told them that.

I'd sat next to him, my knees trembling, my body heating until I could combust.

God, it was so hot.

Then the weather and the room. I had to call Ms. Boyd.

I grabbed a few bottles of water from Gale before I went back upstairs.

Dammit. The key.

I was looking like a fucking noob left and right. The only appendage free was my foot. I lightly kicked the door three times.

He swung it open, his brow cocked. I bet he didn't even look in the peephole. Faced with his broad chest and the way his muscles were clear in the cut of his shirt, I'm sure a robber would have second thoughts. I know I was.

He held the door open. "I see you were successful."

"Gale has got us covered." I set the plates in front of the TV. It was the only available space since he'd moved into the desk. His computer was open, a notepad and pen to the right and a stack of papers and his phone to the left. "I need to call Ms. Boyd—"

"Done. I messaged her a moment ago."

"Oh. Okay. Do you think she'll contact Mr. King—um, your son?"

Gentry's lips thinned and he glanced at his desk, like he wanted to dive back into work but I was blocking the way. "I contacted Beckett as well to let him know he'll have to wait to schedule the interview until we know when we can get out of here."

"Thanks." He'd sounded so grim. What did I do wrong? Had he told Ms. Boyd we were sharing a room with only one bed? That'd be awkward for all parties involved.

I stepped back between the bed and the wall. He lifted another brow.

"You're working. I'm trying to stay out of the way."

"Ms. Brinkley, I think this room will make it impossible to avoid running into each other. You might as well get comfortable." His gaze dropped to my boots, and it was like a vacuum opened between us. My chest grew tight and his expression hardened, but not like he was mad, like he was...

I was being foolish.

"You might as well call me Kendall."

He dragged his gaze back to my face and I struggled harder to draw a decent breath. "Ms. Brinkley will work fine." He grabbed a sandwich and went back to the desk.

I blew out a gust of air. This weather had better pass over soon.

entry

SHE WAS SLEEPING BEHIND ME. I could loosen my restraint and look up into the mirror. The reflection was of an angel. She'd let her honey-blond hair out of its hold and changed into an oversized white T-shirt and loose cotton pants full of cartoon characters. Thankfully, she'd kept her bra on. That shirt would hide nothing.

And I so badly wanted to see everything.

Unlike what my sons thought, I didn't spend *every* night with a different woman. I had dry stretches too. This one was particularly long. Tonight felt like forever.

Since Ms. Brinkley had so thoughtfully brought me food, I'd ignored her. She did the same after my refusal to use her first name. As if formality would keep me from wanting to know what she tasted like, or if that little whimper she'd let out in her sleep was a sound she also made during sex.

Ms. Brinkley with her wide innocent eyes and those bare feet with fuck-me red polished toenails was driving me crazy.

She'd messed around on her phone for hours, tossing and turning, each movement taunting me to stare at her in the mirror. I was very aware of the position of power I was in. She was unemployed and being sent to seduce my son by my mother-in-law.

She wasn't Beckett's type. What was Emilia thinking? He dated women who made a career in front of the camera, be it anchor on the local news or social media darlings that were as famous for their bodies as their number of followers.

Was Ms. Brinkley on social media? Did she follow my son?

I dropped my gaze to the screen. Numbers wavered in my vision. I sighed and rubbed my eyes. Doing this without reading glasses was giving me a headache. Now that Ms. Brinkley was asleep, I could put them on.

As I was digging them out of my bag, Ms. Brinkley's phone lit up and vibrated against the tiny end table.

She sat up and grabbed her phone like she was programmed to do so on the first ring. "Hello? What? No, calm down. What now?"

I tried not to eavesdrop, but it was impossible. In the mirror, she met my gaze and paled. She scooted off the bed and disappeared into the bathroom.

The thin door was no match for her words.

"For heaven's sake, tell Wendell to quit bugging you."

Did Ms. Brinkley have kids? I had no idea how Beckett felt about dating women with kids, but she was so young. Was she married? Had Emilia sent a legitimate applicant and not a prospective bride?

Her exasperated voice drifted right through the walls. "Lenny, slow down. Are Mom and Dad working late again?

What?" The last word cracked harder than a whip. I nearly flinched. When I caught my reflection, I was smiling. I liked seeing that side of Kendall. "When are they supposed to be back? Uh huh. Okay. Put Wendell on."

A few questions were answered, but I had so many more. She was talking to a sibling.

"Wendell." There it was. Her board room voice. "Quit hitting. I don't care if he started it. I don't care if— She said what? Put it on speaker." I wished *she* put it on speaker. How many siblings did she have? "Listen up. I'm out of town. You three need to keep your hands to yourselves and be respectful. I think you can hold out for a few hours. Right? Right?"

I wanted nothing more than to witness this conversation. Meek and quiet Ms. Brinkley didn't mess around with her family.

"Goodbye. Love you all."

I focused on my screen, pretending I hadn't been listening to a thing. Like the kids, all I had to do was keep my hands to myself and then I could part ways with this woman that made me want to know so much more about her.

She crawled back into bed and was breathing deep and even within minutes.

Until her phone rang again. Only this time when she answered, she slipped off the bed and went straight for the bathroom.

"I told you—Look guys, I'm on a work trip. Homework? At this time of night?" Her sigh was heavy enough to make it through the door. "Jen, it's eleven at night, can't you help him? It's only middle school algebra. Fine, what is it? No, you have to flip the one fraction when you multiply, remember. The x is still there. No, not for that. 'Kay? Good night."

Just like before, she snuck back into bed as if I didn't notice a thing. There were several minutes of tossing and turning before she settled down.

I did my own sneaking and got my readers out. Old eyes sucked, but at least reading glasses were all I needed. I could zoom out and see more of the screen. Tomorrow, I wouldn't be driving any farther than to the airport so I could work through the whole night versus trying to catch a wink of sleep in this chair. Because there was no way I was crawling in bed with a woman who might be on her way to get my son to marry her.

It was a little after midnight when I stretched my hands above my head, my fingers interlaced. Another buzz echoed in the room. I took my readers off.

This time Ms. Brinkley took longer to rouse. When she did, she was an adorable mix of sexy and flustered. Her light, soft-looking hair was bunched up on one side and she squinted at her phone. She let out a long exhale and answered it.

"Hello," she said as she staggered for the bathroom.

Was it her siblings again? I didn't have to wait long for an answer. "What do you need money for this time? Can't I register you two for baseball when I get back?" Another sigh. "It's past midnight so the deadline's up. Yeah, fine, I'll try. For both you and Lenny? Make sure you tell Mom to pay me back."

She didn't come out right away. Registering Wendell and Lenny for baseball?

I was turned in my chair staring at the door when she abruptly opened it and marched out. When her gaze landed on me, her cheeks flushed. "Sorry." She dug in her purse and withdrew a debit card then squinted into her phone as she punched the number in. I couldn't take my eyes off her.

All my time with women, I'd watched them get dressed. They cooked for me. They even did yoga around me. But it'd been over fifteen years since I'd watched a woman sign kids up for sports. The nostalgia got under my skin worse than seeing her in skimpy lingerie.

No. Not with her body. The lingerie would definitely affect me more.

Tossing her card back into her purse, she spun and gave me a sheepish smile. "That should be the last time."

"All is well?" I couldn't help but ask. I wanted to know where her parents were and how often she had to take care of her siblings.

"Oh, yeah. This is normal." She tucked her legs back under the blankets and plugged her phone in.

"Why?" The CEO in me wanted answers.

"Um…" She peered up at me from under her lashes. "My parents work a lot."

"How old?" When her brow furrowed, I clarified. "How old are your siblings?"

Her flush deepened. She must've thought I was asking how old her parents were. My pride hoped they were older than me but I was too afraid to find out. "I have a brother that's twenty-seven, a sister that's twenty-three and another that's fifteen. The twins are thirteen."

"Their names?" I should quit talking to her, but now that I started I couldn't stop.

Her face was on fire. She looked away. "Mom and Dad thought it was cute to continue the trend after I was born. Brendell, Rendell, Jendell, Lendell, and Wendell."

Well, they were spread out enough that most people probably didn't catch on. "What are your parents' names?"

"Mike and Susan."

"Interesting."

"It is." She gave me a tense smile before rolling to her side, giving me her back. Well, well, well. Her family was a touchy subject. Or I was just some guy that barely talked to her all day and she didn't see a reason to put up with me any further.

I liked that.

Unless she was ignoring me because she thought Beckett was waiting for her.

As soon as I turned back to my computer the lamp died.

Bedding rustled. The room was dark. Not even the streetlights were on.

"The power went out?" Kendall was checking her phone. "Gale said there's a generator."

The lights flickered back on, then died. We waited a few heartbeats. The room stayed drenched in silence. "Looks like it couldn't handle the job."

"Dammit. My stuff's not fully charged." I checked my computer. It was at twenty-five percent. Damn. My phone. Thirty. Why hadn't I been working with them plugged in?

Because I planned to charge them later. I should've known better in a storm like this.

I kept my cursing under my breath as I prioritized my notes. I had a report to read from the newest geophysicist hire. She was in her twenties and I wanted her insight on the newest innovations. Then there was Aiden's financial report on the North Dakota wells that indicated which ones we should shut down until the price of barrels went up. And I had my quarterly statement to the board. Emilia would have my head if she didn't get a peek at it first.

So that one could wait.

I worked until my computer blinked out, but I'd managed to email myself the innovation report. By the time I was done reading all twenty pages, my phone's battery bar was red.

I shut it off. Best to have some juice for any emergency calls. The room was black. No light emanated from outside and nothing in the room could generate any. I put my glasses away and pinched the bridge of my nose.

Now what? I'd planned to work all night. The temperature in the room had dropped a few degrees, but all that was in my bag were flannel pajama pants and a white T-shirt. I could wear my winter coat to bed. No, not bed. I could drape it over my shoulders and lay my head on the desk.

Yeah, that would work.

The North Face jacket rustled obscenely loud as I eased it out of my bag.

"Are you getting cold already?" Kendall's voice startled me and I froze. How long had she been awake?

"Was I being too loud?"

"No." The blankets shifted and I tried to picture her moving. "I couldn't get back to sleep."

After three phone calls, I could see why. "Don't worry. I'll catch a few winks here."

"At the desk?"

"I don't want to make you any more uncomfortable than sharing a room already has."

She didn't reply. I finished dragging out my coat and shook it open. I was about to toss it over my shoulders when she said, "We're both adults. If they don't get the electricity back on soon, then it's going to get cold really quickly."

It was tempting. Mostly just to stretch out. My shoulders were tight and a steady thrum beat at my temples from all the reading. "I'll be fine."

"All right then. There's two blankets and a sheet. You can get in over the sheet when you decide I don't have cooties."

My chuckle surprised me. It wasn't a bad idea. I didn't want a backache to derail the rest of my busy week. "As long as you're cootie-free, I can get in over the sheet."

She moved again, and the bed gave out a few squeaks. I didn't need light to know she was squeezing as close to the edge as possible.

I felt around until I reached the head of the bed and

peeled back the comforter and middle thermal blanket. Toeing off my shoes, I shrugged my coat off and wadded it up on the end table. Then I crawled in, over the sheet.

The bed was not my normal king-sized one. It was rock hard, had a weird lump in the middle, and was the size of a match box. I could deal with the first two. But the size issue put me too close to a warm lump with a round bottom pointing in my direction.

Suddenly, the creeping chill didn't bother me. I welcomed it and the discomfort it would bring.

 endall

A WARM MAN was pressed up to my back, and I snuggled in more. The blankets were so cozy, but the top of my head was a touch too cold to be comfortable. So I burrowed in deeper.

He was *so* warm. I normally didn't cuddle into Darren like this.

My eyes flew open. I wasn't married anymore. I wasn't even living with him anymore.

It all came flooding back as I blinked against daylight filtering through the window. The storm. Mr. King. One room. One bed.

I rolled over, hoping he was still asleep and hadn't noticed my rabid cuddling. The guy was solid, and I wanted to see what he looked like so badly. Was his hair mussed or was his suit too scared to wrinkle? He'd packed even less than I did. I doubted he had a change of clothes.

I wiggled closer to the edge.

Mr. King's voice made me freeze. "If you get any farther over, you're going to fall out of bed."

"I was, uh, just getting up." I sat up and dropped my feet to the floor. I sucked in a gasp.

"Better find some warm socks, Ms. Brinkley."

A squeak escaped me, and I scurried to the bathroom, snagging my toiletry bag on the way.

There was water, thank God, but it was as frigid as glacier melt. It was fine for brushing teeth, but less fine for washing up. I brushed my hair until it mostly went in the same direction. When I was done, I packed my items and faced the door.

I'd spent the night with Gentry King. I'd slept in the same bed as him. Awkward, party of one.

Shoulders back, I exited the bathroom. Mr. King was up, somehow looking better in rumpled trousers and an untucked white buttoned-up shirt.

His back was to me as he hung his black winter coat on the back of the office chair. The computer was sitting out, and he frowned at his phone.

My phone! I tossed my toiletry bag on my luggage and checked my battery level. Forty. Good. I would only use it if one of my brothers or sisters called and it should have enough life until the power was restored.

Mr. King broke through my relief. "I need to use your phone."

I craned my head around to look at him. "Why?"

His brow furrowed as if his requests were never questioned. "Mine is dead. So is my computer."

I clutched my phone to my chest. "I need to preserve my power in case Wendell calls again." He and I had a special bond and the others usually made him call me. I'd get less vexed if Wendell was on the other end.

The corners of his hard jaw flexed. "I need to find out about roads and flights and check in at work."

"We can ask Gale about the first two."

"She won't know about private flights."

"Unless the whole airport is shut down." I wanted to look outside, but he was between me and the window and I wasn't about to get that close to him.

He steadied his gaze on me as if he was willing me to bend to his needs. "Can you at least check the latest news of the storm?"

"Sure." Now it was a matter of pride. He wasn't getting ahold of my phone and sucking juice out of it. I wasn't leaving my siblings without a way to get ahold of me. I dug my athletic shoes out and stuffed my feet into them. I was in my pajamas, but I had a bra on. I doubted the rest of the guests in the hotel were any different.

I gave him a perfunctory smile. "I'll be right back."

"Ms. Brink—"

I was out the door and smiling. That man stirred my emotions until I didn't know what was appreciation, lust, irritation, or respect. He hadn't done much to earn my respect. Except catch me before I hit the floor at the Billings airport. And make the driver go home. And calmly fire an entire section of employees that weren't adhering to safety standards. And drive through a snow storm like a boss and secure us a room. And then plan to sleep at the desk to keep from bothering me.

All he'd asked of me was to use my phone.

I chewed the inside of my cheek as I made my way downstairs. If Gale didn't have answers, then I'd look it up.

I found her behind the desk, bundled in at least two sweaters and gloves. She was reading a cookbook.

"Morning." She gestured to the replenished table. "I found more bread and grabbed the butter and juice out of the fridge. Sorry about the generator. It passed its last test, but I guess it refused to hold up in a blizzard. Hopefully, the power's on soon, or I'm stuffing the contents of my fridge in a snowbank."

My stomach growled. The least I could do was bring Mr. King some food. But first, I'd find out some info so I didn't go back empty handed in that department. "What's the news?"

"About the same as last night." She lifted her chin toward the door. "It's not letting up."

"You're kidding." I spun to look outside. The only difference from last night was that I could make out the piles of snow. It wasn't just shadowy piles of gray. A steady fall of heavy snow curtained the sky. "Wow. I guess that answers my question."

"Yup. Highways are closed. The plows are struggling through town to keep emergency routes open. I have no idea when we're getting power."

A young couple came downstairs and chatted with Gale. She told them the same thing. I gathered some glasses of juice and made me and Mr. King a few sandwiches. "Thanks, Gale."

"Don't mention it," she said as she directed the couple toward the food.

I knocked on the door again with my foot.

Mr. King opened it, his stony expression inflicting a healthy dose of guilt. To top it off, he took some of my load and put the items on the desk.

Once the door shut, I took a deep breath. "My parents… they had six kids and they're overwhelmed trying to keep their businesses open and raise kids. They've depended on me since I was old enough to change a diaper. They still have three at home, and I make sure I'm around. My brothers and sisters rely on me. My parents rely on me to help with them."

I'd practically raised my siblings. I dug my phone out of my pajama pants pocket and wiggled it. "Can you just check the weather and not use it for work?"

His expression eased. "Of course, Ms. Brinkley."

His insistent use of my last name grated on my nerves. Because each time he said it, his tone caressed down my spine like a low purr.

I held out the phone. "I'll hold you to your word, Mr. King."

The corner of his mouth curved up. He went about his search, moving closer to the window. I rearranged my luggage. There was no use changing, but I found my suit coat from yesterday and put it on over my shirt. And another pair of socks. I looked around. What the hell was I going to do all day?

He approached the bed, his brow drawn down, his face grim. "The local weather station is saying that the snow is going to last all day and through the night."

"Whoa." I sighed. "I'm going to be really late for that interview. I suppose he'll hire someone in the meantime."

Mr. King studied me. "Why do you want…the job?"

I lifted a brow. Something about his tone made me defensive. "Because I don't have one, and I don't have a family empire to pay my mortgage." I let out a sardonic laugh. "I don't even have a mortgage. I don't even have a place to live." I snapped my mouth shut. Had I really said all that?

"Do tell." He picked up a cup of OJ and a sandwich and handed it to me. "There's not much else to do. Playing I Spy will only get us so far."

I smiled and accepted the food, glad he saved the OJ for me. Maybe I shouldn't tell him, but saying it aloud to his handsome face might kick the foundation down on my lust. "Before I was laid off, I lived with my ex-husband. I shouldn't have trusted him and started looking for an affordable place earlier. I should've moved right after my divorce, but Darren was so damn smug about saying I'd probably have to move home." I couldn't look at him. "He always resented how available I am to my family, and he knew making rent would be hard without his income. What I didn't realize was that it was just easier for him to stay, and he likes easy."

Instead of looking horrified, concern brimmed in his eyes. "Where are you staying?"

"I moved back home. Just like Darren said I would." I hated admitting I couldn't afford my own place to a guy who could afford all the apartment buildings in Billings.

"Where else are you applying?"

"I put in a few applications. One at the radio station, in their marketing department. Another at the newspaper. A coworker told me about the position with your son. Well, he told me about an opening, but his sister had signed an NDA and couldn't tell him more."

"It's to marry him."

"Hmm?" I took a bite of my sandwich. Mr. King was still standing by the bed. I didn't think he was a guy who laid around all day.

"Emilia wants you to marry Beckett."

I stopped midchew. "What?"

He finally sat on the bed, his knee kicked up on top as he twisted to face me. "You signed an NDA?" I nodded and made the motion that my lips were zipped. He continued. "My wife set up a trust for each of the boys. But she made certain conditions. And if they're not met, the money goes away."

"There's no job?" I made myself swallow, but my appetite vanished.

"He's looking for an executive assistant, yes. Since Emilia learned of these certain restrictions with the trust, and after hearing that my son's former assistant moved away, she's been sending young, single women to apply."

"But...the trust isn't her money."

"It was. She meant it for the boys, but my wife wanted certain restrictions. It's what happens to the money if the kids don't marry that has Emilia bunched up and gunning for a satisfying resolution."

I shook my head. This was absurd. I needed a job, not a husband. I wanted to work. Getting my childhood back wasn't an option. I'd already raised a ton of kids, now I wanted a rewarding career. The last thing I needed was pressure to seduce my boss. If Ms. Boyd thought I'd do that, did she also think I'd pop out grandkids for her too? "So, I'm stuck in Wyoming with no power and missing days of looking for work?"

He tilted his head. "You don't want to marry Beckett?"

I drew back. "No offense. I get he's your son." And a guy I've never met. "But I have no wish to marry another entitled man who wants me to serve only him and his needs."

Mr. King's eyes lit with amusement. "Beckett and his company are worth millions. I doubt that he'd take advantage of you."

"Well, you're his dad, so you're a little biased. Ask the women he dates."

He chuckled. "He hasn't really been dating. That's the problem."

The air between us eased. He wasn't upset that I didn't want to marry his kid. Any of them. "What's this trust thing all about?"

"I wish I knew." He took a long sip of his apple juice, his gaze boring into the wall. He brought his deep brown gaze back to me. "Sarah was smart and had a good head for business. She didn't want to go into it, so I took the hit and started at the oil company, and I haven't regretted it.

She took over my family ranch. So when her parents sold off a lease holding from the company and gave her half to set up something for the kids, I just told Emilia to have Sarah take care of it. She was in charge of all the home expenses. And she took care of it all right. Divvied it up into a trust for each boy—Aiden, Beckett, Xander, and Dawson. But she added stipulations. They could get the money when they turned thirty if they'd been married at least one calendar year. And if they weren't, then it'd go to our neighbor."

The way he said it told me a lot, but I wanted clarification. "And that's a bad thing?"

He gave me a quick smile. "Losing money is always bad. But losing it to our neighbors is worse."

"Then why did Sarah do that?"

He let out a long breath and studied his juice. "I think…I think she suspected that her parents somehow screwed them over when oil was found."

"*Your* neighbors? How would that happen?"

"King's Creek is a small town. The Cartwrights are our neighbors, and that's a whole different story, but they'd been family friends of the Boyd's for generations. Until oil was found on land they'd purchased from DB and Emilia." He caught my gaze again. When he was looking at me, I didn't notice how chilly it was in the room. "It's not about whose land oil is found on, but who owns the mineral rights to that land."

"Ah." I wasn't surprised. Ms. Boyd had seemed like someone who got what she wanted. "Wouldn't the Cartwrights still make money off the wells?"

"As the land owners, they could charge for access to their land and get compensated for any damages. I'm guessing it was war as soon as the Cartwrights saw what the Boyds were doing with their new oil company. I encounter that behavior all the time. Usually all it takes to resolve is listening skills and more money."

"I'm guessing the Boyds were short on both when it came to their severed friendship?"

He got a faraway look in his eye. "Probably, but since Sarah's dead because our bastard neighbor Danny Cartwright hired a drug riddled criminal that everyone told him to stay away from, I really don't care."

"Oh, Mr. King. I'm sorry."

"I suspect Sarah thought the chances of all four boys fulfilling the stipulations was low and somehow money would make its way to Danny's daughter. She always had a soft spot for her." He shifted his gaze to mine. "Each trust is a lot of money, Ms. Brinkley. It would solve all your problems and help your family."

"I want to help them, but I also want my own life and career. I think I've earned it." Hurt curdled the peanut butter in my gut. Was he trying to marry me off?

"You'd get half when you divorced. That's one of the stipulations. It's pre-nup exempt."

"Can they even do that?"

"Sarah did. It's a hundred million dollars. You'd get fifty."

I sputtered. "Holy *shit*. That's a ridiculous amount of money. Who even has that much?"

He shrugged like *who doesn't?*

"Gah. I just—No. Quit suggesting it. I want a job not a husband. Not even if it's just for a year."

"Was your marriage that bad?" He took another bite of his sandwich.

"At first, it didn't seem like it. He was fun. Carefree. Not burdened by five siblings. He was my escape. Only he wasn't an ounce of support."

"Did they call you at all hours of the night when you were married?"

I flashed him a guilty smile. "Yes. And then I had Darren to take care of too. He said he didn't feel cherished enough."

"Didn't he discuss how he felt with you?"

"If by discuss you mean passive aggressive comments that made me feel small and like my family is full of parasites, then yes. I'm sure he'd complain that I was always working or on the phone too much for us to have a real conversation. I had to pay for liking my job and loving my family." I hadn't liked my workplace, but I enjoyed the actual work I did. "I get that I spend a lot of time running my siblings to appointments and going to their plays and games and performances. But I doubt he would've been happy if I saw them only twice a year."

"Never apologize for it. Not for helping your family, not for loving to work." He put his empty cup down. "Thanks for bringing me food."

His easy acceptance of my circumstances in a couple of sentences was more support than Darren had ever given me. "Gale might have a deck of cards."

He looked at me like I was speaking foreign words. "And just what card games do you play?"

"What? Because I'm a Millennial I don't know how to play cards?"

There was that arrogant assessment again. "What card games do you play, Ms. Brinkley?"

This time he was playing with me. I leaned forward. "Go. Fish."

He laughed. A real laugh that vibrated sinfully through me and showed me his laugh lines. It only made him more handsome.

"What about you?" I asked.

"Rummy, gin rummy, War. Slapjack, Crazy Eights, Blackjack, poker, Texas Hold 'Em, and Canasta."

"Canasta? Isn't that an—"

His gaze sharpened, the air growing charged between us. "An old person's game?"

"And old *lady's* game."

That got another chuckle out of him. "Sarah used to play it. Winter in Montana before the internet was so easy to get in rural areas."

"So, that's why you have so many kids," I teased.

His brow crinkled as he shot me an incredulous look. "It took us a while to figure out what was causing it."

My giggled sputtered out. "You learned quicker than my parents. Just kidding. They call themselves good Catholics, but bad at natural birth control." I didn't want to leave. Our conversation was getting good. "I'll go see if Gale has set out games. She thinks of everything."

"I'll come with. I need to stretch my legs."

entry

I WAS HAVING FUN. Straight up fun. And I still had my clothes on.

Kendall flipped a card, and I slammed my hand down. "Got it."

"Ohmigosh, Lightning McQueen." She tossed the jack of diamonds on the discard pile. "You're crazy fast. I've officially lost."

We sacrificed some heat for light and opened the thick curtains. The limited sunshine managed to brighten the coffee-brown carpet. Since there wasn't much else in the room other than dark grain furniture and abstract art with the same coloring as the flowers on the bedspread, I'd take all the light I could.

It was Kendall's turn to shuffle. I sat back on the bed and watch her hands work the cards. She was grinning, her head partially tucked into her puffy coat and a brown stocking hat on her head. Our room was cool, but it was warmer up here than down in the lobby where the picture windows let in as much cold air as light. Gale let the guests borrow games as long as we brought them back after a few hours to trade out with new ones. We weren't the only ones looking to pass the time.

She started dividing the cards into two even piles. Her phone had died an hour ago. "How about a good old-fashioned game of war?"

"You think you might have a chance to win?"

She grinned and looked up at me while she dealt. "There's gotta be one game I have a chance at."

"My kids were ruthless, but Sarah played for keeps." I'd never talked about my wife as much as I had in the hours since we woke. It felt comfortable. Kendall didn't get awkward about my late wife like others did.

"After meeting Ms. Boyd, I can believe it." She nibbled her lower lip. "I probably shouldn't talk like that."

"I'll do it for you. Emilia's a force, and not always a positive one. And don't worry, I've told her plenty of times."

She thought for a moment and then shrugged. "Well, I guess it's not like I'm ruining my chances at getting a job. I'm not pursuing the assistant position."

"Don't get me wrong, Beckett would be a fair boss and pay you a good wage, but you'd be married to the job even if you weren't married to him. He flies all over the country, sometimes the world, on short notice."

She sighed wistfully. "Somedays, I wouldn't mind. I always wanted to travel, but between the cost and taking care of my family…"

What she had said about her siblings surprised me. It was one thing for her parents to take advantage of her while she lived under their roof, but another to do it so far into adulthood. And now she was under their roof again. She'd admitted it had affected her marriage, but it sounded like with her winner of an ex-husband that its demise was eventual.

But I expected taking care of her family was more than an obligation. It was a challenge. They kept her busy. Her career hadn't met those needs so she allowed her family to fill in.

Her former boss was a fool to let her go. I knew it without seeing a scrap of her work. I'd hired enough people in my time to know when they would be excellent employees or not.

"Have you thought about applying to King Oil?"

The cutest little line developed between her brows. "Would I be qualified?"

"I don't know. What do you have for ideas about the company?"

She cocked her head, our cards sitting forgotten between us. "I think your concentration on what the company does for local communities is admirable and a good choice, but I think you could also highlight what King Oil is doing about its carbon footprint."

"Not many people know that an oil company cares about the environment."

Her smile was sly. "I'm sure when it's good for the bottom-line, they will. It looks good to the public."

"Looking good for the public is important. Their opinion influences our investors until their decision to invest is less about the oil and more about how we're handling other energy sources."

"Do they know you fund a lot of research with wind energy?"

"They do, but not many others know about that. You've done your research."

A light flush brushed her cheeks. "Not many people are

told they're flying alone on a private jet with an oil CEO. Why doesn't more of the public know that King Oil is so involved in wind energy?"

"I'm working on it."

She nodded. "I get it. Communicating with the masses is different than a colorful graph in a meeting."

She flipped a card out and I did the same. Mine was higher. I shot her wicked grin. I won the battle.

She narrowed her eyes and we continued playing. "It was interesting actually. I never thought about oil other than seeing your company billboard all over. Nice branding, by the way. You can play on the word a lot more too. Why'd the name change?"

"King had a better reputation than Boyd." I'd never talked so much about the company with someone who wasn't family. Most didn't care, or just wanted to talk money. "Emilia is business smart, but stubborn to a fault. And a little impulsive, but she always has her eye on the end product. Her husband DB wasn't quite as savvy. He also wasn't subtle or clever in his dealings."

She gave me a dubious look. "Ms. Boyd's not subtle either."

"Exactly." I pushed a card out and she matched it with one of hers. We both flipped at the same time.

Mine was a two of spades. Hers was a three of hearts. She grinned and grabbed both cards. We continued playing.

When was the last time I was this comfortable with a woman? I wasn't working on charm, or congenially trying to extract myself from a warm bed I no longer wished to linger in. We were playing cards in a snowstorm.

To keep conversation going, and because I liked hearing her voice, I asked about her siblings. Her stories brought back memories. My youngest was twenty-six. Not much younger than Kendall, but we managed to share similar parenting experiences.

"Middle school is rough," I said after she described how Wendell's anxiety attacks returned in sixth grade. "Xander refused to talk about it, but when he'd get home after school, he'd do chores and then disappear on his horse for a couple of hours. I talked to all his teachers. There was nothing going on, he wasn't acting out, and nothing bothered him."

"What was it?"

Our cards were forgotten between us. "I assume it was how he was dealing with his mother's death. They all had their different ways, and...I had my own that they didn't approve of." I'd never be able to forget Beckett's eyes welling over with betrayal when he first caught me with a woman. Sarah had only been gone six months.

Having sex again didn't mean that she was forgotten. Every time I was around one of the boys, I saw all the things she'd miss and how much of her each one of them had woven into them. Sex had been an escape, a reminder that I was still living and my own person, one who was more than dad and oil CEO.

"How old were they?" Kendall asked quietly.

"Aiden was thirteen. He's the oldest and they're all about a year apart. I'd say they went wild afterward, but I think they had that coming anyway. Aiden closed up on himself, Beckett took his rage out on me, Xander shut down, and Dawson cooked."

"He cooked?"

I nodded solemnly. "That kid could get into Le Cordon Blue if he wanted."

"You did good with them. I looked you all up when I heard who I was interviewing with."

"I was good with them at first. Once they were teenagers,

they didn't need me around as much anymore." That was a harder pill to swallow than I had anticipated.

I was telling her more than I'd ever told anyone—about my kids, my job, and my wife.

A grown man should be able to count on friends, but I'd never had many. I ranched with my parents and after they moved to Arizona, I hired people. They weren't friends, they were employees. At the company, I was the top, my son was my second, and more employees. The women I dated were all kept at a distance because I wasn't looking to settle down.

But this friendly chat, Kendall's banter, was new. And nice. She was easy to talk to and nicer to look at.

So, I kept reminding myself of her age. Not yet twenty-nine. The longer I was around her, the more insignificant it seemed.

"Should we see what Gale has for lunch?" She stretched. The coat bunched around her breasts. The woman didn't know how devastating her curves were. She slumped and frowned. "Though I feel bad she's raiding all her supplies to feed us."

"I'll reimburse her." I gave Kendall a pointed look to wipe out her guilt. "For all of us."

"For all—" Her eyes went wide. "For the whole hotel?"

"It's a small place, but it could be the Hampton we stopped at first and it wouldn't be an issue."

"That's really generous."

"No use having this much money if I'm going to stash it under my bed and leave it there."

Her stunned expression turned dreamy. "I'd love to know what that's like."

"Maybe you will someday, Ms. Brinkley. Shall we go down and see what's for lunch?"

∾

WE PLAYED Scrabble for two hours. Kendall's vocabulary and talent with seven letter tiles was impressive. Then came a game of Sorry, and she didn't even have to look at the instructions. It was growing too dark in the room to play anything that would require light.

Gale had given each room a flashlight. There was no news about when the power would be back on, but the temperature had stabilized. We didn't quite see our breath, and if we huddled on the bed in our winter gear, it wasn't miserable.

Since no one else could play in the dark we didn't bother to run the Monopoly game downstairs.

Our dinner was day-old donuts. My doctor would hate my diet the last couple of days. Growing up dining on the fattiest cuts of meat and then working in a career that demanded a lot of travel and quick food didn't play well with my genetics.

She glanced at the window. "I don't think it'll be a comfortable night of sleep."

"No." There was no way I was offering up the idea to share body heat. For one, I didn't want to make her uncomfortable. For two, I didn't want to make *me* uncomfortable.

The afternoon hadn't increased my friendly feelings. Instead, I realized she wasn't wearing an ounce of makeup and her lips were a pale pink, unless she nibbled on her bottom lip. Then it turned magenta. Her two middle bottom teeth turned toward each other as if they were cuddling up like she did to me this morning. When she smiled, her right eye closed just a little farther than the left, and every quirk I learned about her only made me like her more.

I'd woke before her this morning and hadn't moved. There was nowhere to go and nothing to do but listen to her even breathing and feel her lush body pressed into mine.

What a way to wake up.

Then there was her laughter. She giggled and almost

seemed embarrassed. When she snickered, it was after besting me in a game. And her full-body laughs with her head tossed back. I lived for those.

She yawned and huddled in on herself. Gale had passed out extra blankets that we'd saved for the night.

"We might as well crawl under the covers," I said.

She nodded and started spreading the extra blankets out. One was a quilt, an old-fashioned tie one where each block was a different color. The other was a heavy gray blanket.

She used the bathroom first, and then I did. The water was cold, but with all of us using it, the hotel's pipes should be safe from rupturing.

I got into bed under the blankets only. She crawled in between the sheets.

We were quiet for several minutes before she spoke. "I really didn't know I was expected to marry your son."

"You weren't." I stared at the dark ceiling. "You were expected to be so captivated with him that you'd seduce him and he'd want to marry you."

"That's messed up."

"Yes. But that's Emilia's thinking. Not Beckett's. He's a good kid."

I could tell she wanted to ask something. I didn't have to wait long. "Do you think he's going to try to marry, just to get the money?"

"I don't know. None of us want the Cartwrights to get it. Danny Cartwright is a mean drunk, and he'd use that money to buy up everything around our land. He'd buy out businesses and bribe people. It's enough money that he could destroy the town."

"If he stayed sober enough."

"He has a daughter. Bristol's younger than Dawson, my youngest. If Danny drank himself to death she just might finish the job of destroying us for him. There's no love lost there. Which is too bad. It wasn't always like that."

The bed moved like she rolled to face me. "The families were close once?"

"Not Danny and us. But Sarah took Bristol under her wing whenever she could. When Sarah was little, she used to be best friends with Danny's sister. I think she saw a lot of his sister in Bristol. Sarah always had a soft spot for Danny, even after the rift. Everyone thought Sarah would end up a Cartwright."

"She dated him?"

"Not quite. I think she cared for him, but he never got the nerve to ask her out. I'm sure his parents forbid it after the mineral rights drama. Then Sarah and I started dating as seniors, and Danny started hitting the bottle." I let out a deep breath. Maybe it was the dark. Maybe it was Kendall, but all kinds of things I never told anyone spilled out. "She got pregnant as soon as we messed around. Aiden was born before either of us turned nineteen."

"And you stayed together and kept going?"

"We were a team." There went my mouth again. "I was going to take care of her and the kids, but once she told me she was pregnant my life was decided. DB and Emilia didn't allow for it being any other way. At least we were compatible." I sensed her confusion. "Don't get me wrong, we loved each other deeply, and as long as I was married there was never anyone else. But that's why my kids have reacted so harshly to my lifestyle. They don't understand."

"Don't understand what?" The bed shifted again like she propped herself on her elbow. I stayed on my back, staring at the black ceiling.

"They had each other. I loved Sarah. We married the weekend after high school graduation, but then she was gone and I had no one. I started sleeping with others, and once I worked through my grief that way, well, then I was still fairly young and single."

"You weren't much older than I am now," she murmured.

"Don't get me wrong. I don't regret it. Not at all. But I regret how my boys interpreted it. But how could I explain it as reclaiming my younger years without diminishing what Sarah and I had?"

"Maybe they'd understand now?"

I shook my head. "No. Those years before she died were idyllic for them—and for me, really. I'll never take that away."

She reached over and squeezed my arm through the many layers. "You're a good man. And a good dad."

I blew out a gusty breath. "I don't know. Aiden married a really nice girl, and I'm afraid…" I snapped my mouth shut. It was one thing to talk about me and my life, but I couldn't share Aiden's details.

"You're afraid he married her for the money?"

"With me as his role model, he thought it was perfectly fine."

"Oh, Gentry. He saw more of you than that."

Was it when it counted though? The question dominated my mind more than hearing her same my first name. "I've quit that lifestyle. It's over."

"So, you're like…"

"Abstaining." And I was feeling it. Being around her made me count the seconds since my last time coming in a woman. But then I could hardly remember the moment or the person. I should've known I had a problem long before Aiden's wedding. "I haven't been with anyone since my son announced his wedding last summer."

"And by doing that you hope to spare your other kids from thinking women are tools?"

"I never thought women were tools, but I never had to lie or make promises to get them in bed."

She snorted. "You wouldn't have to."

"The money."

"God, no. Well, yes, I'm sure for some. It's your looks. You're hot, Gentry King. You know that."

"I…guess." My looks weren't something I dwelled on. I tried to stay in shape so I didn't have heart issues like my dad. But when I started this trip, I thought Kendall would be mesmerized by my son. Not by me.

"Since we're being so forward, I can't believe Ms. Boyd didn't cause trouble and forbid you to be with other women."

"You and me both. She didn't condone it, but she looked the other way. Honestly, I always wondered why." Kendall could read people. It probably only enhanced how good she was at her job. I was convinced now more than ever that her old boss was an idiot.

"Do you think it's because of your neighbors? If your wife had married that guy instead, she might've been ruined by his lifestyle."

"In the end, she *was* ruined by his lifestyle, but I know what you mean. He would've found his way into the bottle eventually, and she would've suffered a lot longer than a few hours." Such a huge weight had lifted from me that I felt like I could float off the bed. "I've never talked to anyone. About any of this, especially about her."

"I've never talked to anyone about my family. I've had one boyfriend since my divorce, and it was short-lived. The sex wasn't worth having to hear him complain about the late-night phone calls."

I chuckled. "You have your priorities straight. Don't feel bad about that." It wasn't just her boss that was an idiot. I was convinced that Kendall Brinkley was surrounded by them. Her old boss, her ex, that quickie boyfriend. None of them saw her for the treasure she was. They only wanted to use her.

"He was one of my oldest brother's classmates, but he reminded me so much of Darren. And I was lonely. But then he got irritated when Wendall called one time at midnight all worried about a band performance. He gets stage fright and I help him breathe through it. I mean, he's getting better at dealing with it on his own, but he's just starting his teenage years. I left that guy's place and told him not to call me again."

I would've done the same if one of my boys called that late. I had done the same. No one but me decided when I would or wouldn't be there for them. "There's nothing wrong with walking away if it doesn't feel right."

"Gentry." Her voice was growing sleepy. This time, hearing my first name on her lips hit hard. I wished I could curl around her, winter coats and all, and just hold her. "I'm glad it was you I was snowed in with."

"Likewise, Ms. Brinkley." Likewise.

 endall

I WAS ROASTING. So freaking hot. I squirmed, not fully awake, kicking off my blankets. That voice saying my name. *Ms. Brinkley*. I was achy. Needy.

There was a man in bed with me, and I *wanted*.

So hot. I wiggled around, seeking relief, but I'm not sure from what. The heat? The ache between my legs?

"Ms. Brinkley."

I was baking. A whimper escaped.

"Ms. Brinkley."

"Yes?" My voice was breathless. A dull throb centered in my body and I let out a long moan.

"Kendall." His voice snapped me out of my restless sleep.

I opened my eyes with a gasp. The lamp was on and the room was warm. Blankets were strewn all over the floor and Gentry stood on his side of the bed. I blinked at him. He'd taken off his cold weather gear and changed from his suit into pajama pants and a white T-shirt that sinfully hugged his body. The shirt didn't hide much. I made out defined pecs and solid abs in the dull light.

Had I made a fool of myself in front of Gentry King? After he decided to look at me and talk to me, he revealed a strong, witty, and compassionate guy who loved his family and worried about them every moment of every day.

"The power's on." I was stating the obvious but I was glad I said something more than *take your shirt off, I wanna see*.

"It's been on for a while."

I sat up. I had a few layers to strip down. "Couldn't sleep?"

The muscles flexed in his jaw. "It was...hot."

I ducked my head, sheepish. "Oh, sorry."

He waved me off. "I have a lot of work to catch up on."

My heart sank. We couldn't be stranded together forever, but yesterday had been fun. "Right."

"I plugged your phone in."

"Oh. Thanks." I checked it for missed calls. There were three, all from Wendell, and a message that told me to never mind, he got ahold of Ren to help with his homework.

I squinted at the time. Four in the morning. Gentry was quite the workaholic. I stripped off my coat, then my gloves and socks. "I should grab a shower."

I was rushing to the bathroom, but Gentry stopped me. "I'd be surprised if there's hot water yet. And other guests are going to be using it."

I'd been sweating for who knows how long, and even though it was hours before dawn, I'd gone two nights without more than a frigid spit bath. "I'll risk it." I went to my suitcase and dug through it. "Um...would you mind terribly if I wash out my underclothes and hang them to dry?"

My cheeks burned, but I had one dirty pair of underwear and the pair I just sweated in.

His lips twitched like he was going to grin. "How about I do the same and you won't feel so exposed."

"The couple that hangs their underwear together?" Why did I have to say that? The artificial light seemed more like a signal to go back in time to our stilted reaction to each other.

His smile put me at ease. "We bared our souls, now we bare our underwear."

Grinning, I disappeared into the bathroom.

After scrubbing my clothes and losing hope for a warm shower, I went ahead and turned the water on. There was only enough warm water to make it tolerable, but I got my body and hair washed.

When I left the bathroom, I intended to fold the extra blankets, but Gentry had already done that. He was back at the desk.

"Did you get any sleep?" I asked.

"A few hours. I'm fine."

I caught a peek at his monitor. The font was huge. Didn't he have reading glasses?

Yes. He did. "You can wear your readers. I won't think you're a geezer."

His gaze lifted and pinned mine in the mirror. "What gave me away? The forty-eight font size?"

"Quit lying. That's fifty-two."

He laughed. "Busted. My readers make me feel old."

"So do my knees when they ache before a rainstorm." I crawled into bed, my eyes growing heavy. I was warm and clean and didn't have to worry about draping myself over Gentry. "It happens to all of us."

"Good night, Ms. Brinkley."

And he was back to that. "Good night, Mr. King."

I don't know what my future held, but while I was in this room with him, I didn't have to worry about it.

When I woke several hours later, Gentry was still at the desk.

"You're still working?" I stretched and rolled to my side. What time was it? "Can't you take a storm day?"

"I haven't really taken a day off since I handed the ranch over to Dawson. And with the power outage, I'm quite behind."

"Can you delegate anything to your assistant?"

He rolled his neck and flexed his shoulder muscles. "I have an assistant who arranges my schedule, but not an executive assistant. Emilia only allows family into what she calls the inner office."

"Neither you or your son has a direct assistant?" When he nodded, I sat up, stunned. "That's too much work for each of you. You need time off, and an assistant."

"If I told you what I was paid, you wouldn't think it was too much." His back was to me as he clicked through pages on his screen.

"You're paid for the amount of responsibility you have and the magnitude of the decisions you make. Emilia needs to butt the hell out and retire." The more I heard about her, the more I disliked her. Finding out she had sent me off like chattel didn't help either.

"Agreed. There are muffins by the TV for you. Gale's been cooking up a storm."

He did the food run? Of course. He needed to know the weather details. "What'd you find out?"

"The roads are getting cleared off, but snow totals are twenty-six inches, so it's going slow. The airport probably won't open today." He sighed and took his readers off. "Even if the airport opens, the crew is stuck at Shirley's aunt's house. She lives too far out of Douglas to make it to town today, or even tomorrow."

I whistled. "We're really stuck."

"Yep." His phone buzzed. When he looked at it, his expression shuttered and he answered. "Emilia."

My heart stammered. I hadn't been able to inform her that Denver was a no-go. To keep from feeling like I was eavesdropping, I found my muffin and dug in. A cup of OJ was next to it. He seemed to know that I preferred orange juice over apple juice. Or that was all Gale had left.

"We're still stranded in Douglas... I don't know, you'd have to talk to her... Emilia." His voice took on an edge. "You can talk with her about the job. Ms. Brinkley is a professional, and don't think I don't know what you're trying to do." He eased against the back of his chair. "No. Of course not. It's not like that. Emilia." He caught my gaze in the mirror. The anger he was suppressing made his eyes fathomless. "I have to get to work. Did you get the board reports I forwarded?"

He delved into oil speak and I was interested in hearing, but my phone went off. The number was unfamiliar. "Hello?"

A deep voice asked, "Ms. Brinkley." The same intonation as Gentry. I knew immediately who it was.

"Yes."

"This is Beckett King. I understand you were on your way to interview for my executive assistant position."

I snuck into the bathroom so I didn't disturb Gentry and his conversation. "Yes, Mr. King. I've been waylaid in Wyoming by a storm."

"With my father."

"Yes." I bristled. He sounded so disapproving.

"I can assume you're no longer interested in the position?"

I wasn't, but I didn't care for what he assumed. "Why would you assume that?"

"Ms. Brinkley, we don't need to pretend—"

"Mr. King, I'm no longer interested in working for you. My decision has nothing to do with the snowstorm and who I'm waylaid with."

His derisive snicker inspired instant anger. "I doubt that's the case."

"Actually, you're correct. I was under the impression that I was applying to be your assistant. I never would've applied for that job if I knew that your grandma was playing Tinder."

"Ah, let me guess. You found a bigger payday in my dad. Spoiler alert, he doesn't commit. You'll be left broken hearted with no extra money, nothing more than what you started with."

How dare he? *"Spoiler alert*, Mr. King. You're being extremely insulting to both me and your father." I wanted to tell him where he could shove that position of his, but I couldn't risk Gentry overhearing. This was still his son.

"Really? Did you get separate rooms while stranded?" I took too long answering. I shouldn't have to give him an excuse. "I thought so. Goodbye, Ms. Brinkley."

He hung up, and I held the phone, staring at it. I kept my growl under my breath and whipped the door open.

Gentry was on the other side. He looked me over as if to check that I was physically okay. "That was my son."

He wasn't asking. Emilia must've called Beckett King before she dialed Gentry. I nodded.

"And he assumed that you and I slept together."

"Don't forget that I'm using you for your money."

He gave one nod. "Emilia assumed that I used you for a distraction."

I leaned against the doorjamb. "You did, you know." When his surprised gaze landed on mine, I nodded. "You used me to play War. Gin rummy. You even played an extra round of Slapjack knowing that I have the reflexes of a sloth."

"I was giving you a second chance."

"Bullshit, Mr. King."

He fought a grin. "Language, Ms. Brinkley."

I looked him over. His face was lined with fatigue and after hours and hours of reading on his computer, he probably had a headache. "Why don't you lay down for a while?"

"I have—"

"Work, yup." It was my day to interrupt the Kings. "How can I help?" He was shaking his head but I crossed my arms. "Find something for me to do and get your butt in bed."

Heat smoldered in his eyes but he shut it down. Not before I saw. "I'm not one to argue when a woman wants me in bed."

I straightened the sheets and blankets. By the time I was done, he was ready and standing beside the office chair. "Have a seat, Ms. Brinkley."

"These are some marketing pitches from my team. Look them over and give me a summary of them all and your opinion."

"What else?" I gave him a droll look. "This will take me an hour. Maybe an hour and a half. You need more rest. What else?"

His lips quirked. "Fine." He leaned over me, and clicked out, choosing a file labeled geophysics. We'd been in bed together, but there were a lot fewer layers between us at the moment. "Here's a file from my new geophysicist. She's also one of the youngest I've hired for the level of position she's in. It's created an...issue."

"Between her and the older guys that don't think she has anything beneficial to add."

"Seems you know the drill, Ms. Brinkley." He lifted his chin toward the computer. "She's a professional, but I also wanted her insight on the cultural shift that her age group is bringing to the workplace. You'll have the same insight as well. Read her stuff, and then her supervisor's opinion, and tell me what you think."

"You've already done that."

"Yes. My forty-eight-year-old self has. I need another opinion to help me forge ahead. There's only so much interpreting data I can do before I have to make some changes."

As long as it wasn't just busy work, I was mollified. I shooed him away.

He paused for a moment. Still close to me. "Thank you."

"It'll be my pleasure to work with a boss who isn't a schmuck."

He chuckled as he climbed into bed and I got to work. It seemed that whether I worked for him or talked with him or played games with him, it was all a pleasure. And the longer it lasted, I only wanted to experience more with him.

CHAPTER 10

 entry

I WAS MORE relaxed than I'd ever been. Without waking fully, I could tell I was sleeping on my side, curled up in a way I hadn't done since I was a boy, since before I worked cattle all day and collapsed in a heap. Definitely before I was handed the helm of King Oil and given the responsibility of the wealth of some small countries and a whole slew of people's careers.

For once I didn't feel alone. Because I wasn't.

There was someone else in bed with me. She was quiet and close, but not touching. And I didn't mind. I liked her there. I'd grown to look forward to the moments I was in bed with her, dreading it as much as I lived for it.

Like last night, when she made sounds that made me wonder what she was dreaming about, *who* she was dreaming about. I'd had to get up to work, even though I'd stayed in bed after the power came on. It took a while for the room to warm up, but I'd been content to stay next to a bundled-up Kendall.

Ms. Brinkley.

Opening my eyes, the view I saw made me think no, I wasn't going to jump out of bed and get to work. She was lying next to me, also on her side, facing me. Her eyes were closed, lashes a few shades darker than her hair brushed her cheeks.

This wasn't the first time I watched her sleep, and I never did that. I hadn't met anyone I was willing to slow down for.

You keep your greedy hands off her, Gentry. She's for Beck.

As if Kendall was a hundred-million-dollar heifer. Emilia thought she could still salvage the job interview, but I knew both my son and Kendall better than her. Neither one would want to work together. He wouldn't trust her, and she didn't really want to move away from Billings.

She opened her eyes as if sensing that I was thinking about her.

A sleepy grin transformed her face from ethereally beautiful to sex goddess. Her lips were full and her cheeks pink, her hair spread wantonly around her.

"Did you get some rest?" Her sleep roughened voice only made me wish I was the cause of it. I bet that's what she sounded like after loud, hard sex.

"Yes. Did you lose interest in the assignments?"

She shot me a playful scowl. "No, they're done. I didn't want to do anything to wake you up so I thought I'd lay down for a while."

"They're all done?"

"You didn't give me anything hard or time consuming. I even took the time to write up my opinions and ideas so you had record of it. I have to say that what you do is fascinating.

You'll have to work harder to find something to really challenge me. Might as well if we're stuck here."

I was interested in what she left me. Really interested. Emilia was strict about who was allowed into the inner office, and she wasn't someone I could turn to for insights like this. She'd lose it if she knew I'd let Kendall do as much as she did. I wasn't sitting on state secrets, but Emilia didn't realize that information was often better shared in order to gain a broader understanding that would benefit the business. She came from a business mindset that those who controlled the data wielded the power and each leak was as bad as a gusher in the pipeline.

I let my gaze wander over Kendall's features. She was doing the same to me. What did I look like to her? Too old? Young for my age? Did she wonder what I looked like when I was thirty instead of pushing fifty?

"You're going to let me help you more, right?" Worry tinged her question. She wanted to help. Sitting in this hotel room while I worked until we were cleared for takeoff would drive her crazy. I could read her so easily and we'd only met a few days ago.

"Kendall, I will let you do whatever you want."

A slow smile stretched those mesmerizing lips. "You called me Kendall."

I couldn't help myself. I shifted until I was closer and did what I've wanted to do for days—found out if her skin was as soft as it looked. Stroking my fingers down her cheek, she was better than I imagined.

My body roared to life. It'd already been half-mast waking with a woman, but it knew it was *her*.

Her eyes widened, then she closed them and rolled closer to me. "Gentry."

It was my name that knocked down my restraint. I could tell when a woman was attracted to me, and Kendall wanted me. I wanted her. My mind refused to remember why this wasn't a good idea.

I leaned in and pressed my lips against hers. Softly. We were still lying side by side.

Then she whimpered, just like she did the other night. Needy. Aching.

I needed more. But I was under the covers.

With a growl, I kicked them off and took our kiss deeper. She opened for me, her tongue warm, inviting me inside. She tasted of sweet orange juice. It was her favorite. I didn't have to ask. She always set it closer to herself as if hoping the extra few inches would make me bypass it. Noticing things about her had become my new favorite hobby.

Surging over her, I wedged one leg between hers and like the kiss, she opened for me. Gently settling my weight on one arm, I used my other hand to stroke her hair back. Her kiss was greedy, demanding, and I gave it to her. Licking and nibbling, I suckled her lips like I wanted to play with her clit. I took it fast, then slow. Firm and soft, finding out what she liked.

She was so responsive. Her hips arching up when she especially liked how I tightened my hand on her hip. And the way she swayed into me as I swept my hand up her torso until I cupped her breast through her shirt.

She was a perfect fit. With one of my legs between hers, we were completely aligned. I held myself off her enough to flick my thumb across her pebbled nipple. I was rewarded with a low moan, just like she did when she was tossing and turning in her sleep. What had she been dreaming about in those few moments between deep slumber and wakefulness?

I wasn't too young and foolish to hope it'd been me.

I loved playing with her pert nipple, but I wanted to touch skin. After a full day of her being covered from head to toe, I needed to find out if her skin was as smooth and velvety as it looked.

Brushing my hand down, I tried to keep enough distance so I wasn't crushing my dick between us. I was painfully hard and more turned on that I'd been for months. Years. Sex had become nothing more enjoyable than a snifter of brandy. A little fire on the way down and then I was over it and wanted to get home and back to work.

But I didn't want to go anywhere right now. On top of Kendall was the place I've wanted to be since I first caught her in my arms. Since I rounded the corner out of the office to see her fine ass ready to hit the floor.

I hooked my fingers around the waistband of her pajama pants and tugged down. They wouldn't go far with my leg acting as the stopper, but they lowered enough for me to recall that her underwear was hanging in the shower. She wasn't wearing any.

My own groan matched the extra discomfort of even more blood pouring into my erection. How could she be so sexy doing something as simple as washing clothes?

My fingers brushed across her fevered skin and my questions were answered. She was soft but strong and so incredibly hot I wanted to burn up in her atmosphere. I was so close to her center, so ready to find out if she was as ready for me as I was for her when the vibrating of her phone distracted me.

She released my mouth with a gasp, her wide teal eyes locking onto mine. I didn't want a fucking phone call to interrupt us.

"I'm—I'm sorry." She rolled over to answer it.

Reality slammed into me.

Fuck.

I'd crossed the line with a woman I shouldn't want. Emilia wouldn't believe me that Kendall had lost interest in the job. My boys would think I stole someone who'd been interested in one of them. They'd think my claims of abstinence were bullshit and continue to shut me out of their lives. They'd throw the age difference back in my face.

I rolled off the bed and stood with my back to her, hearing her talking to Wendell, or Lenny, or Jen.

"Brendell, that's amazing. Congrats. Have you told Mom and Dad? Aw, you're sweet. Thank you."

Stuffing a hand through my hair, I slammed my other hand on my hip. What did I do? I couldn't take back what we'd just done and go back to handing her a report to read or playing a round of Uno. I also couldn't tamp down how badly I still wanted her.

Why did the one woman I truly fell for have to be the one who could unravel my life?

"Gentry?" she asked tentatively. "Are you all right?"

"No, Kendall. I'm not." So much for Ms. Brinkley. I couldn't pretend that the formality helped me keep my distance at all. "That shouldn't have happened. I'm sorry."

"Why?"

I looked over my shoulder as if she was speaking an alien language. "You're too young."

She had the audacity to roll her eyes. "No, I'm not. Look, I'm not going to beg for your attention. I like you, and if you don't like me, then say it. But don't go blaming age or that we're stuck in a one-room hotel or some other irrelevant excuse."

I wanted to turn around and speak to her. But then I'd be reminded that she wasn't wearing underwear. Why the hell was that kryptonite for guys? It's not like underwear was a steel girdle.

I pinched the bridge of my nose. "I like you, but that doesn't mean I can do this. My kids think I'm a misogynistic predator that uses women like disposable wipes."

"Why would your kids find out we were together?"

I stared out the window at the piles of snow. Plows had built mountains of the stuff along the side of the road and a few brave motorists were out. The scenery didn't give me hope that we'd get out today. "They'll think it since you told off Beck. And I don't lie to them."

My erection had flagged enough that I could turn around without flashing a tent in my pants like I couldn't control my damn body. Which I couldn't seem to do around her.

Her features tightened and hurt darkened her eyes. "Oh. I see. It would've just been a fling for you."

"I don't do relationships."

She chewed the inside of her lip and looked away. "It's better that we don't do anything then. So you can be honest with your kids. I don't want to get in the way of you repairing your relationship with them."

I'd have to let her think that. I couldn't tell her that nothing about this felt like a fling. She was funny, dedicated, smart, and getting to know her would be an honor. Hell, I'd gone to school with Sarah my entire life and our decision to date was just that, a *why haven't we done this before, let's try it out* kind of thing. After Sarah was gone and I'd been single for a while, I'd wanted my freedom.

But I wasn't free. Emilia looked the other way regarding all the women I'd been with. They didn't threaten the company, and I performed at my job. She might even have enough of a soul to feel guilty for dictating what my future would be as soon as we told her that Sarah was pregnant.

Whether or not a relationship would bloom out of having sex with Kendall wasn't the problem. It was my last conversation with Emilia.

She's a nice girl, one that I thought Beck would actually like. If you fucked it up because you touched her, I won't hesitate to fire you and rebrand this company like I did before.

It wasn't her threat to me. I could walk away and live an easy life with what I'd made over the years. I could buy my own island if I ever wanted to leave Montana. But I wasn't going to saddle Aiden with that stress when I worried about how he was doing under it in the first place.

So, it ended up being about my kids anyway. I'd have to accept loneliness in order to stick around and help my kids through the tornado that was their Grams.

 endall

MY PRIDE HURT, but at the same time it glowed. Yesterday, Gentry wanted to use me for sex. I'd seen the women that had been on his arm and there was no reality where I felt like I was in the same realm as them. Tall, svelte, and gorgeous, they'd all looked like they had more sophistication in their pinky finger than I possessed in my plain, white-bread body.

After my oldest brother called to tell me the good news that he and his wife were expecting, Gentry had backed away like I was a poisoned apple and he'd been close to his teeth piercing flesh. A delicious quiver ran through me. It was a heady experience for me. I couldn't persuade Darren into a quickie before Monday Night Football was over. Gentry had acted like he lost his mind around me.

I didn't quite believe he wanted nothing more than sex. It might be a pipedream to think I was above all his other hookups, but we had a connection. A burgeoning friendship at the very least.

Ultimately, he didn't want to be with me, and that stung more than I anticipated. I hadn't scared him off with three days in pajamas and the bed hair and the Arctic explorer look, but our time together talking and sharing our life stories hadn't made him think there was a future for us, or that he even wanted to explore the possibility.

Go, me.

So, I'd spent the time while he was working doing some research on my phone. Job hunting. Then I went down to grab some food and talk to Gale for a couple of hours. All while he was working.

He sat on that damn computer and ignored me the entire time.

Today was a repeat. Only this time, Gale told me the diner down the street was open if I wanted a hot meal for a change.

I was in the bathroom, brushing my hair and putting a dab of mascara on so I'd stand out from the snowbanks in some way. Next was getting on something that I hadn't slept in. I chose the outfit I wore here. My second set of business clothes would be worn whenever we got to leave Douglas.

When I was done, I went back out and stepped into my boots. I was zipping them when Gentry's hard tone made me pause. "Where are you going?"

"Gale said there's a diner a block away that's open." Finished with my boots, I put my coat on. It wasn't in bad shape for having been slept in.

"Do you mind if I go with you?"

My heart surged, but I kept a neutral tone. "No. You're welcome to come along."

"Kendall…"

"Maybe Ms. Brinkley is better." That was cattier than I

intended, but after the hottest kiss of my life and the quickest brush off, I was allowed to be a little bitchy.

"Give me five minutes," he said quietly.

I nodded and sat on my side of the bed as he disappeared into the bathroom. When he emerged, I looked at him once and glanced away. He'd put his charcoal trousers and white button-down shirt back on, but the top button was left undone and his sleeves were rolled up to his forearms. Tanned skin with a scattering of small scars made his arms more than simply *arms*. They had character, and his muscles flexed with every move.

He saved me by putting his own coat on. "Ready?"

The way to the diner was as quiet as I expected. Gentry and I didn't talk. Most of the sidewalks had been shoveled. Not all the businesses were open, but they probably looked out for one another, clearing the walkways and sprinkling salt.

The temperature was just below freezing, and the stroll was almost pleasant. And bright. I squinted ahead. The sun was out, and its force was reflected all around by fresh snow. If we had to walk any farther, I'd be snow blind.

I snuck a peek at Gentry and wished I hadn't. His eyes were narrowed and his lips were firm. He probably thought the fine lines around his eyes revealed his age, and I guess they did, but they were sexy. He was distinguished, and those lines only added to his intensity, the intensity that I hadn't realized had left when we played games on the bed. He'd been so relaxed. Did anyone else ever see him like that?

The diner was half full, and the fresh-cooked greasy food smelled amazing. I wanted all the burgers and fries. A waitress Gale's age seated us in a corner booth. It was the kind of diner where the napkins were in a bin on the table with the ketchup, mustard, and menus and I wouldn't get a fork unless the waitress thought I needed one. My favorite.

Gentry didn't bother looking at the menu.

"Know what you're going to have?" Did he have a personal chef? A home delivery system? Or did he eat out?

"I never have to decide at a place like this."

I raised my brow. That was arrogant.

He mimicked my move but his tone was teasing. "A patty melt and hashbrowns."

For a guy that had crazy amounts of money and resources at his disposal, he didn't act much different than any other businessman. In fact, he seemed less picky than the entrepreneurs and CEOs I'd worked with before. He didn't complain about the peanut butter and jelly sandwiches we'd had two days in a row or about the steady diet of muffins, day-old donuts, or cookies that came after.

"But I shouldn't," he said.

Maybe he was pickier than I thought. "Why not?"

He winced like he regretted he'd said anything. "My dad has health problems."

I was stunned by both his honest answer and that he'd even said it. "What kind?"

"Heart. He started with high blood pressure and then last year he had a double bypass."

"You think it's genetic?"

The corner of his mouth kicked up. "I don't want to find out. And I'm getting to the age where I will."

"I can't imagine the stress you're under helps."

He shrugged it off as if it wasn't a major contributor to high blood pressure. That's what all the commercials said. "I work-out every morning. That helps."

It was weird to be on the receiving end of the health worries talk. At my old job, my female coworkers would talk about various health issues and insecurities, and often I'd join in. It felt like what I should do. But none of the guys had contributed. Maybe they held it all in, thinking they shouldn't talk about it.

I liked that Gentry did. And I'd be willing to bet that he only did it with me.

He shared something so I threw him a bone. "My brother's having a baby. That was why he called."

"Are you excited?"

"Yeah, actually, I am. It's a kid I won't have to take care of, and I think he'll be a good dad. His wife is definitely sister approved."

"Does he help you with the others?"

I took a sip of my water. "No, he has no problem drawing a line, and his wife enforces it." The waitress stopped by. Once our order was out of the way, I decided to keep pushing how open he was.

"Riddle me this, Gentry King." His brows lifted, but amusement lit his eyes, with a healthy dose of wariness. "You have a load of money. You can buy anything. But you love a good ol' diner patty melt and you thrived on PB and J and apple juice I'm pretty sure was from concentrate."

"And you're wondering why I'm not an entitled prick?" When I nodded, he smiled. "Many would argue I'm quite entitled."

"You know what I mean."

He nodded. "I grew up slinging cow shit. It wasn't because the ranch wasn't lucrative, but because my parents believed that in order to appreciate what I had that I had to work for it. I did the same with my kids."

"And your youngest took over the ranch?"

"He knows what to do to keep the business well into the black, and he also knows how to do every task King Ranch requires."

I didn't know much about ranching, but it seemed like a lot for one family. "Didn't you hire people."

"Yes, and Dawson has two full-time employees, but it's a business where knowing every facet and whether it's being done correctly and efficiently can make or break an entire operation."

It should be harder to picture the guy in the suit across from me out slinging manure or whatever he did growing up, but that body wasn't manufactured in a gym. "That's how you kept ranching while working for the company."

He stretched his legs out and crossed his arms. A look that was so at odds with the tycoon vibe he gave off with the way he was dressed. "It needs to be a pretty sizable operation to raise a family on. Often one spouse works full-time, just for the benefits. Sarah preferred to ranch." A nostalgic smile ghosted across his lips. "It was like we traded places for a while. I worked for her family company, and she worked for mine. When she was gone, the boys picked up a lot of slack."

I kept peppering him with questions about his life and he didn't hesitate to share. We'd slipped back into the comfortable relationship that both of us seemed to crave. But it didn't change how much I wanted to be more than friends.

I HADN'T MOVED at all since I woke up. Gentry was pressed against my back with his arm around my waist. I was happy to let him stay like that, but I warred with myself. He wouldn't want to be wrapped around me like a second blanket. He wanted to face his kids with a clear conscience.

After lunch yesterday, he'd given me more work to do, and I hadn't begged. He had stayed at the desk, and I had stretched across the bed. Then I'd settled in to sleep. I don't know when he climbed in bed, but he was over the sheet and I was under.

His arm tightened around me, then stiffened. I tried to stay relaxed and breathed evenly.

"You're awake."

How did he know? "Does that make me a bad person?"

He sighed, his nose nuzzled in my hair, but didn't move. "No. I would've done the same thing. I was thinking, there's an entry level marketing position open in the Williston office."

"I'd have to move to North Dakota?"

"Yes, but it's closer to home than Denver."

My family was in Billings. "I was willing to move to Denver when I first lost my job, but now that I've had time to think, and I have a niece or nephew on the way, I'd like to stay close to home. If possible. Besides, don't you think Ms. Boyd would have a problem if I'm hired?"

He tensed briefly before he said, "I'd take care of Emilia."

Then he'd have to deal with Aiden and Beckett. Who knew what the other two sons would think. "Thanks for the offer, but I'll keep looking."

He rolled away, taking all his heat with him. "I'll see if we're getting out of here today."

Nothing was said about our morning spooning, or the hard length that had pushed against my ass through all the layers.

He ended the call with "See you at ten."

Our time together was over. We took turns cleaning up and we were packed and ready.

At the desk, Gale grinned. "You get to break out?"

"Yes, ma'am." After she processed the payment, he pulled out his wallet and dropped more hundreds than I could count into Gale's hands.

She stood frozen, her hands out. "Oh, no, Mr. King. I can't take this."

"You didn't stop even when the storm did. Please use it to restock your pantry and give yourself a break."

She laughed and gave him a wink. "There's not enough for that last part." She shook her head and stared at the money. "This is just…thank you."

We left a stunned Gale behind. It took both of us to brush the snow off the SUV. When we finished, there was a sizable pile outlining the vehicle. I was able to see the sprawling town on the drive to the airport, not so different from a Montana small town.

The flight wasn't any different than before, other than Shirley's excited stories about the storm and her reaction to our stay—Gentry omitted the part where we were in the same room. Gentry didn't sit on the other side of the plane this time. He sat across from me, passing me the tablet he'd kept on the plane and discussing various reports.

Before we touched down, he handed me the tablet again. "Enter your information so I can pay you for all the work you did."

Pay me? "I didn't really do much—"

"Kendall, you worked for me for three days."

"Partial days."

"Regardless, you're getting paid for it and for your time."

I should stick to my principles and argue with him, but I was broke and would be picking up the early morning shifts at the diner this weekend. I had to save up money to move and that would be painstakingly slow on diner tips. I entered my account numbers and punched them in. "Thank you."

"It's the least I can do."

We landed, and once the door opened, Gentry hung back to deal with the crew. I stepped outside to go down the short stretch of stairs and cold air slapped me in the face.

Here I was. Back to reality. Time to find a job.

CHAPTER 12

entry

"WHAT THE HELL IS THIS, GENTRY?" Emilia stormed into my office, slamming the door behind her. I hoped Aiden had gone out for lunch like he usually did. His office was next door, and with her voice raised to the level it was, he'd hear everything. "What is this about a marketing position getting moved from Williston to here? For *Kendall Brinkley?*"

"I've done my due diligence through Human Resources." And I'd used my status to secure the position for Kendall.

"Did you fuck her?"

I took a steadying breath and remembered who I was dealing with. Interactions with Emilia took a little finesse. Arguing with her got nowhere. "No. I didn't." I sat back in my chair and leveled my gaze on her. "But since we had so many days together, she wanted to work. She's good, Emilia."

Emilia rolled her eyes. "Good at what? She got fired from a low-level marketing position."

"Her talents were untapped. She was fired based solely on having less education than her coworkers."

Emilia's right eye twitched. I thought that would get to her. Much like Sarah with me, Emilia had met DB young and got pregnant. She'd married him and they were partners in everything, but she had to work ten times harder based on her gender and that she'd stayed home to raise Sarah while DB went to college. If there was one thing she'd didn't tolerate, it was writing someone off because of their level of education.

"She was supposed to be for Beck."

"Listen to yourself Emilia. She's a person. Her family's in town and they rely on her."

Emilia pressed her polished lips together. "You seem to know a lot about her."

"We were together for four days."

She narrowed her eyes. "And you didn't touch her."

I eased out a breath, but kept my composure. "Not that it's your business, but no."

"Why didn't she want the job with Beck? It's a good job."

"Her family's in town and her brother's expecting. She decided she wants to be around for them."

"She's his age." As if that was a job qualification.

"Beck will find someone if he wants to, Emilia."

"Not soon enough." She dropped into the chair across from my desk. I sighed. I was already working through lunch, now I'd get behind even more. If it wasn't for Kendall's help, I'd be working through half the night.

She rubbed her temples. "What's he waiting for?"

Not this again. "Probably to meet someone and fall in love."

"Happy marriages can happen with less."

"There's still time."

There was a knock on the door that connected my office to Aiden's. He walked in. How much had he heard?

"Grams." Aiden leaned down to give her a perfunctory kiss on the cheek.

"Aiden. How's Kate?"

We all knew she wasn't asking because of genuine concern over Kate.

Aiden indulged her with a smile. "Still married to me."

Emilia beamed up at him. "That's my boy. You always do right by this family." She tilted her head and slid her gaze to me. "I used to be able to say that about your father."

Aiden's smile faded. "Something wrong?"

I answered instead. "The woman she wanted to farm out to charm your brother was snowed in with me."

"In the same room," she added.

Aiden lifted a dark brow, his expression darkening.

"Nothing happened, other than seeing what a brain we'd be missing out on if we didn't snatch her up."

"You stole her from Beck?" There was my oldest. Always sounding disapproving of me.

"No. She expressed her lack of interest in the position when it was clear that her family in Billings needed her." And that it was more like a pre-arranged marriage than a job.

Emilia settled her stare on me and I reverted back to the eighteen-year-old in her living room, getting told how my future would go. "So much so that he moved a position from Williston to Billings."

"Because she still needs a job. I'd rather have her talent working to make this company money than hitting send on resumes. She did some work for me in the hotel room. I've seen how good she is firsthand."

Aiden studied me. "Are those the funds sitting on my desk waiting for approval? For a Kendall Brinkley." The request shouldn't have had to go through Aiden and he was astute enough to read the irritation in my expression. "The supervisor wanted it approved by both of us. Your reputation precedes you."

An approval from both of us? That wasn't our policy. The insinuation became clear. "She thought I was using the company to pay for a prostitute?"

Aiden kept his gaze steady. "It's an unusual request."

"Approve it. Kendall did the work and sacrificed four days for a job she didn't know was supposed to lead to a marriage proposal."

"And a hundred million dollars," Emilia said.

"Or fifty million if she divorced him after a year," Aiden said wryly and my shame was renewed. How could he take this lightly? "What kind of work did she do?"

I gave Aiden my hardest stare. "Pay her."

A subtle narrowing of his eyes didn't escape my notice. It wasn't often I pulled rank, but that made twice so far for Kendall.

"Gentry." Emilia rose. "For the first time, I'm starting to wonder if maybe you need to retire."

Aiden's eyes flared. So, he wasn't the unfeeling bastard he wanted everyone to think. Running this company alone, especially with Emilia possessing the power she did, would ruin him.

I was tired of Emilia's games, but the best tactic had been to idly play along. "Maybe after I go help Dawson this weekend, I'll agree with you."

There was the eye twitch. She didn't want to return to the company and function as the CEO any more than I wanted to quit. But I knew better than to push her too far.

EMILIA WAS GONE, but Aiden lingered. He crossed the door between our offices and I thought that was it. But he closed the door and came back to my desk, taking a seat.

I settled back. Now what?

His expression was placid, which for him looked like he was angry as hell. That was him. He scared more people than he comforted. "Tell me about this Kendall Brinkley."

"Why?"

"She's going to be working for us. She obviously made an impression."

Did he think he could fool me? "What are you really asking?"

"Is she hot?"

"Yes." I wasn't going to bluff about her looks. "Why do you think Emilia thought she'd win Beck over?"

"Interesting."

"Is it."

He studied me. I was used to his type-A ways. His need for control and meticulous style made him perfect to take the helm of this company in the future. But I'd grown weary of being on the receiving end of it.

He kicked an ankle over his knee and leaned on the arm of the chair. "Why didn't you sleep with her?"

"I meant it when I said I was going to change. I didn't approve of what you did to Kate."

"Married her and gave her a life with anything she could ask for?" His tone was flat.

"I never saw what I did before as using women, but I see the error of my judgment, just like I saw how it influenced you."

His expression darkened. Kate was an off-limits topic with him. It gave me hope. He was either ashamed of what he'd done, or he cared for her. I hoped for both, but I wouldn't know until he turned thirty and was free to divorce her and keep the money away from the Cartwrights.

"So, you wanted to sleep with her. But you didn't?" He made it sound like an improbability.

"You want honesty, Aiden? Yes. I wanted to sleep with her. As soon as I saw her. She's cute, she's sexy, she's smart, and she treats me like a normal person. It's intoxicating. *She's* intoxicating. But I was resolute about my decision to quit dating and there was no way I was going after someone who might be interested in one of my sons."

Aiden tilted his head, true confusion in his eyes. "And what about when she decided she wasn't interested in the job, which I have my doubts about."

I leaned forward, putting my elbows on my desk. "She turned out not to be interested in being set up with your brother, or she would've interviewed, but I doubt she would've followed through. She's dedicated to her family. And your brother was a jackass on the phone about it."

"Why? He doesn't like Grams shoving women off on him."

"Because he thought she found a bigger payload in me."

Aiden snorted. "As if he thought you'd be interested in someone enough to settle down."

I blinked at him. I wanted to argue, but he was right. I hadn't wanted to settle down any more than I wanted a prostate exam. I still didn't want a cold latex covered finger up the ass, but the idea of settling down wasn't as undesirable as before. Not when I remembered sitting in pajamas, bundled up on the bed and playing cards.

"I kissed her and that was it. I stopped it there. It was a mistake."

"But she wanted to keep going?"

The way she'd looked at me before I'd touched her. Her eyes hooded and her face flushed. The softness of her skin still made my hands long to hold her again. We had fit perfectly together. "I think so. It didn't matter. It *doesn't* matter. She's too young."

He nodded like it all made sense. "She wanted to get a job here."

"You think that's the only reason why she was interested in me?"

His cockiness amplified. As if he'd decoded the opposite gender. "You could be her dad."

I'd been a kid when I'd had him, but it didn't change that he was right. "No, she didn't think applying here would be a good idea because of your Grams. If she accepts the position, give her a chance to show what she can do before you write her off as a user."

His steady gaze remained on me for a few beats past comfortable. "Why'd you move that job out here? At one time, she was willing to move to Denver. Why not Williston? She might've done work for you, but you can't know how she is in marketing without references."

Wasn't that a million-dollar question? Why not offer it to her first and see if she'd move somewhere a little closer to home? But I'd been like a man with a purpose, organizing the transfer. "She was unfairly fired and helps her family." She lost her job, but she'd charged her brothers' baseball fees. I couldn't let that go.

"It isn't going to be easy," he said softly, surprising me that he actually sounded concerned for someone. I lifted a questioning brow. "It's going to get out that you paid her a special wage for unknown services and then modified a position so she works under the same roof as you. You haven't damaged the reputation of the women you actually did sleep with like this."

"People can assume what they want."

"People can, but Ms. Brinkley has to work for them."

"Let her know she can come to us with any issues." Which

might make it worse. Shit, why didn't I think of that? "She'll have a probationary period like anyone else. Mrs. Chan is her manager. I doubt I'll even see her most days."

Aiden made a noncommittal noise, as if he assumed either me or Kendall would go out of our way to see each other.

Would she?

Would I?

I couldn't. People wouldn't take lightly to her having a direct connection to me. No, I'd already done enough harm to her professional standing. The best thing I could do for her was to stay far away.

endall

MY FIRST DAY OF WORK. On Friday, before heading into a weekend of applying for jobs, after a week of lackluster interviews, I'd gotten two bursts of good news.

The first was a notification from my bank that a deposit had been made. A sizable one. One that left me beaming and vexed at the same time. I wasn't a charity case, but damn did I need the money. The amount was close to a month of my previous wages. The paystub I'd been emailed indicated that it was prorated based off an oil CEO executive assistants' salary.

If that was close to what other executive assistants made then I should've followed through on that job with Beckett King.

But no, I had no wish to be in the middle of that level of family drama, especially if it involved Emilia Boyd.

Brendell had stared at me when I'd beelined into his

office and asked for help moving my stuff from my parents' to my new apartment.

The next burst of good news was getting a call from King Oil HR. There was a distance-based entry level marketing position open and I came highly recommended. I didn't have to ask by whom, and after an interview where the guy interviewing me looked at my legs more than my face, I also didn't want to push my luck. I accepted immediately.

Smiling to myself, I collected my things and got out of my car. King Oil headquarters loomed in front of me in all its glass-walled glory, reflecting the sun in a way that made the building look like the rich brown of fresh oil. It was four stories tall, and the crown on the emblem that made up the "O" in oil was unmistakable branding.

I strutted inside, my stomach a flurry of tumbling nerves. Would I see Gentry? Had he dived right back into work and forgotten about me? It'd only been two weeks since our time together. I was sure he was the one behind my recommendation for this job, so he hadn't completely forgotten about me.

At the reception desk, I gave my name and waited until the receptionist called someone named Mrs. Chan.

A woman with short black hair and appraising eyes walked out, her heels clicking on the tile. Her navy suit was impeccable. I felt like a cluttered discount bin facing her in the boots and skirt I'd worn on the flight to Douglas.

She gave me a pleasant smile. "You must be Kendall. I'm Mrs. Chan, the marketing manager for King Oil."

"Nice to meet you."

She nodded once and turned, indicating for me to follow her. "Come. I'll show you to your office and get you started on the HR paperwork and videos. That'll take up most of your day."

I looked forward to it and the challenge of learning a new job.

She took me up to the third floor. When the elevator doors opened, I expected a Herman Miller cubicle farm like the one I'd worked in earlier. There were cubicles, but not like I'd ever seen. The walls were much higher and not set as small, squared-off boxes. They were curved and earth toned, using the deeper browns and taupe that accented the exterior of the building. As Mrs. Chan led me by them, I saw people on exercise ball chairs, standing desks, and treadmill desks.

But when she led me to my office, my mouth dropped open. It was a real office. In the corner, facing out the back of the building, overlooking the outskirts of Billings. A walking trail wound through the lawn and at the far edge were remnants of cattails that must mean there was a damn pond on King Oil property.

"This is nice."

An unreadable expression flitted through Mrs. Chan's eyes. "Yes. It is."

My computer was already on, and she walked me through passwords, training courses, and had the forms I needed to fill out already downloaded.

When she apprised me of enough to keep me busy until the end of the day, she rose. "The break room is down the hall. I can take you around and introduce you to the team before break and show you where everything is at." Her lips pursed. "And introduce you to the rest of management."

Did that include Gentry? Or Aiden? Did everyone here call them Mr. King, and did it get confusing? "Thank you."

I was about to turn back to my screen, when she closed the door and faced me. "I hate to bring it up before you even have a chance to begin, but I wondered why Mr. King moved a position from Williston to the home office." She speared me with her direct gaze. "But then I heard about the trip to Douglas."

I recoiled. What? So everyone here thought I got the job because I slept with Gentry?

I didn't have a chance to ask before she continued. "Just know that I'm trying to be open-minded and not scrutinize your work more than any of the others, but you will be held up to the standards of everyone else."

"I'd expect no less," I said stiffly.

She feathered her fingers over her hair, the conversation seeming to bother her as much as it did me. "He's never done this before with any of his others and I can't argue that there's no reason this couldn't be a distance position, but it would've helped if you were around your actual team for a while."

He'd never done this before? So now, not only did everyone think I got this position because I had sex with Gentry, but that I must have a golden pussy as well. Was that better or worse?

"Mrs. Chan, I didn't sleep with Mr. King." My cheeks burned and I feared someone would jump out and yell *liar*. I slept with him a lot. Fully clothed. I refused to think about the kiss. "But while we were stranded, I offered to help him with work since I had nothing to do."

She cocked her head and I was reduced to being a bug under her lens. "I certainly hope that's the case. I hope you impressed him with your skill and knowledge and that's why he bypassed other more highly qualified applicants."

Could he do that? Legally? He must've. Otherwise the news of me being hired wouldn't have spread so fast.

She pointed to the phone. "Dial 301 or shoot me a message if you need anything."

I glanced out the door as she left. Humiliation swaddled me like a prickly blanket. I wanted to crawl out of my skin and into the nearest black hole.

He's never done this before with any of his others. Getting up,

I went to my door and closed it. I needed more than a few minutes to face everyone in this building, including Gentry.

~

BREAK CAME WAY TOO SOON. Mrs. Chan knocked on my door and popped her head in. "Ready to meet everyone?"

No. Absolutely not. "Yes, thank you."

Getting shown off on the first day of a new job always ranked as the most uncomfortable experience in adult professional life. Today, a healthy dose of steroids was dumped into that experience.

I greeted everyone, forcing myself to stand still under their inspection. It was like I could hear what was going on in their heads. *She's the one he did this for? I bet she doesn't know a lick of marketing. Will she disappear into his office for nooners?*

My face burned so hot, I feared the top layers of skin would peel off.

Then to make things worse, Mrs. Chan led me to the elevator. "Time to meet Aiden and swing by Mr. King's office."

Now I knew how to address each of them. "Does Ms. Boyd have an office here too?" When I met with her, she'd met me in public, at a restaurant.

"She doesn't work too often anymore, with the exception of board meetings. Most things have been turned over to Aiden and Mr. King." Thank goodness. "But she's in today."

For fuck's sake. I wasn't catching a break at all.

The fourth floor was blinding. Light streamed in all the windows, unencumbered by cubicle walls. A desk with a young man in a cornflower-blue suit sat in the middle. Each corner had a door and there were a few desks making up a waiting area by the assistant's desk.

"Morning, Phillip."

Phillip grinned. "Happy Monday." His gaze landed on me and I stood still for his perusal. "You must be Ms. Brinkley. You guys can go on into Aiden's office. Mr. King just took a call."

Mrs. Chan's gaze flicked to me, as if she was assessing my giddiness over getting to see Gentry again.

I wanted to bolt when Mrs. Chan swung open the door to Aiden's office. This was the guy who couldn't stand his dad's lifestyle and had used his wife to throw it back in Gentry's face. What the hell was he going to think of me?

A younger version of Gentry sat behind an imposing desk. He looked up, his expression unchanging. I might as well have been another stack of reports. His face was more angular than Gentry's, and his hair had a cowlick on the right side that had probably been adorable as a kid. His desk was sparse, save for one photo by his phone. His wife? I couldn't tell.

The pictures on his walls looked like Montana countryside, but farther east where it was flatter.

"Aiden. This is Ms. Brinkley. Have you two met?"

His intense scrutiny was focused on me as he stood. He was a couple inches taller than Gentry, and while Gentry had a lean and muscular frame, Aiden was stockier, if that term could be used to describe someone who towered over everyone.

"I haven't, but I've heard my father rave about your work."

"Thank you. I plan to surpass the compliments."

He lifted a brow in a move that could be construed as arrogant, but I didn't get that impression. Everything about Aiden's demeanor could be written off as conceited, like the way his upper lip curled just a little. But I think it was just him.

"Good to hear. You're from Billings?"

"Born and raised."

"My wife works at the library. She's our age. Kate McDonough."

He married a McDonough? I'd heard he'd gotten married, and then only what else Gentry had told me about it. But not who. The boys in that family were on a first-name basis with every law enforcement officer in Billings, and probably the sheriff's office and highway patrol as well. I vaguely remembered the McDonough brothers had a sister. She was quiet, a book nerd, and a real wallflower.

"I think I'd recognize her if I saw her, but I recall nothing but good things."

That earned a hint of a smile. Perhaps he wasn't using Kate. I didn't get the impression he smiled much, unless it was good for business.

"Let me see if my father is off the phone." He crossed to a door that connected his office to Gentry's and just walked on in.

I couldn't see Gentry, but the offices looked similar.

"I believe you've already met our newest employee." Aiden stepped aside, like a big reveal. *Here's the woman you slept with, and we all know it.*

Gentry's gaze lifted from his screen. His expression could be considered pleasant but there wasn't a smile ready to happen. "Ms. Brinkley, welcome to King Oil."

"Thank you, Mr. King." There. I was just as cool and collected as him even if my insides were roiling. His suit jacket hung on a hook by the other door, and his pewter shirt only made his shoulders look impossibly wide. I'd seen him in business clothes on a private plane and in a hotel room, but I couldn't picture him as a desk guy until now.

There was no doubt he owned the space. The giant windows behind framed a Montana landscape that had seemed to form especially for him. His office overlooked the walking path and park behind the building. His office was also directly above mine.

My cheeks warmed. He'd been directly above me once before. Then it was all over before we got started.

He turned his focus back to his computer. We'd all been dismissed.

Hurt reflected through me. What did I expect? That he'd ask about Wendell and Lenny's baseball? Or Brendell's baby?

Mrs. Chan's smile was tight but her eyes were relieved, as if she'd expected Gentry and I to eye-fuck each other. "Come. I'll show you where the break room is."

I looked toward Aiden to thank him for the welcome, but he was eyeing his dad with an introspective expression. Gentry had made him sound like a hard-ass, but he'd been the most congenial one I'd met. Mrs. Chan didn't radiate hostility. More like a "fine, if I have to" attitude about training me.

I followed her out. Aiden trailed behind me.

I hadn't realized how much I'd read into this position until now. That Gentry more than liked me as a person. That he couldn't forget me. That our short make-out session had meant something. I knew my place now, and it was nowhere near Gentry King.

entry

A MESSAGE POPPED up on my screen. I usually ignored the notices. After all this time, I could tell if it was important or not in the periphery of my vision. This one caught my full attention.

Sender: Kendall Brinkley.

I hadn't seen or heard from her in the three weeks since she'd been my employee. I pulled up her message.

I wanted to thank you for paying for those hours worked in Douglas. It wasn't necessary, but since you did I was able to secure an apartment. And thank you for the job.

That was it. I wanted to know more. Had her brothers started baseball? Was anyone giving her problems with the job? Was she free Saturday night?

None of those answers were my business. I could ignore her email. I *should* ignore it. Not many lower level employees emailed me directly unless they were given approval by their manager. But Kendall's supervisor was in North Dakota and I hadn't spent four days with any other employees other than my son.

I swept the cursor over the delete button. It hovered there.

Dammit. I typed a reply. *You're welcome.*

I was about to hit send when I recalled the hurt simmering in her eyes after my curt dismissal of her in my office after she's started working. Telling myself it was necessary didn't make it better, but I also didn't miss how Mrs. Chan seemed satisfied that I didn't roam around Kendall like a prize bull looking to mate. Aiden had looked at me like he'd never seen me before.

I added, *How's the job going?* Before I lost my almost forty-nine-year-old nerve sending a woman an email, I hit reply.

There. It was done.

But I couldn't go back to work. I watched the wave of dots that told me she was replying. Fuck the reserve reports. I waited.

It's good. Really interesting and more than what I went to school for. I didn't realize how stifled I was at my old job. I'm even going out with some coworkers tonight.

So much for Aiden's fear.

Have fun. I paused. Giving up my internal battle, I typed, *Have the twins started baseball?*

Just the workouts and practice, no games yet. The smiley face after her words only made me imagine her grin and how her teal eyes lit up. Then I compared them to how dark they got when she was in my arms and under me.

Aw, hell. The pressure was back. My blood headed south. Not again. Just when I was getting to a point where I didn't think about her every second. I was going to have to go out for a few drinks. No plans to pick up any company, but a delay to keep from jacking off in the shower, alone, on another Friday night. Good thing no one told my teenage self that things didn't change much by the fifth decade.

The next words I typed flew out of my fingers and my thumb hit enter before I could stop it. *Dawson played ball and we have a lot of land if they ever want to practice. I could give him a call.* King's Creek was a couple of hours away. What the hell was I thinking?

The wavy dots held me captivated. When her reply hit, I started to laugh. *Please tell me Dawson's not turning twenty-nine soon and this isn't a setup.* I heard the words in her wry tone.

Promise. No hidden agendas. But if Emilia ever invites you out...

Then I'll tell the twins. My parents' yard is the size of a stamp.

One of the Christmas special ones?

Haha. Sorry to be bothering you. I wasn't sure a message would be welcome.

I took a measuring breath. This conversation was all kinds of trouble, but it was exactly what I craved. *I don't want to fuel any more rumors of us.*

I think they're already soaked with gasoline.

Which was all my fault. *How's it been really?*

Mostly good. It's getting better. The first weeks are always awkward. My coworkers are taking off. I'd better go—we're carpooling. Have a good weekend, Gentry!

I was Gentry to her again. I couldn't deny I loved the starched way she said Mr. King, but it was also a reminder of the separation between us.

I reread our missive a hundred time before I forced myself back to work.

It was getting close to eight. I wrapped up some emails and glanced over at the door to Aiden's office. The light was on underneath.

I went to the door and tapped on it as I walked in.

Neither of us ever waited for a response. One day, I hoped to catch him in flagrante with his wife, not because I was a pervert, but because that'd mean they had something real. Aiden was scowling at his screen. The top button of his shirt was still done up tight and not one hair had moved the whole day. He was as ready for the day at eight thirty p.m. as he was at seven thirty a.m. And I'm sure he finished a punishing workout before he hit the office.

"Why aren't you at home?" I asked.

He didn't bother to look up. "Kate has a late-night meeting at the library."

Doubt snaked through me. Both of them working late? Or was one lying? Since I was standing across from Aiden, that would make Kate, which was absurd.

"A late night at the library?"

My dubious tone got Aiden's attention. "It's game night for the teens and she stays around to help."

I sat across from him. "Does she want kids?"

He rolled his eyes. "We've only been married five months, Dad."

"Legitimate question."

"She hasn't mentioned a thing."

"Maybe if you were home, she could."

He pushed away from his computer with a huff. "I have a job to do, Dad. If I don't do it then thousands will be out of work."

Sounded familiar. It was the story I gave him while he was growing up.

Can we play ball, Dad?

No, son, I have a lot of work to do.

"You can do your job well and still have a life," I said.

"Is that what you did?" he asked flatly.

This wasn't going anywhere. It never did, and since he'd gotten married, it got hostile faster. I rose and headed toward the door. "Learn from my mistakes, Aiden. Don't emulate them."

I didn't bother to shut the door. I left it open, hoping that'd force him to get out of his chair and that'd start the cascade process of heading home for the weekend.

I was getting my suit jacket on when he appeared in the doorway. "You know I only have this job because I'm your son. Anyone that made the mistake I did would be lucky to get the swing shift at a shit factory."

Ah. The mystery that was my son was unraveling. He never talked about the incident from when he'd first started with King Oil. "It wasn't a mistake. It was a decision that didn't pan out the way you thought."

"And a lot of people lost their jobs."

"And they got unemployment and found new ones. Don't destroy yourself over it."

He looked like he wanted to say more, but he just shook his head and walked away. I counted the day that financial mistake was discovered as the second pinch point that changed him from the oldest child with a wealth of ambition and a witty sense of humor to a hard, driven man that left his emotions in the dust. The first pinch point was the night his mother died.

I needed a drink.

It was Friday. Rodrigo was working. He wouldn't ask questions, but I could still talk to him. About nothing and everything without saying anything at all. He was the second best person to talk to. The person I really wanted to visit with was out with friends.

I LEFT both my overcoat and suit coat in the pickup, draping them over the back seat. The tie had been ditched as soon as

I'd gotten behind the wheel. It was still early spring and cool, especially at night, but the cold hardly penetrated my Oxford shirt.

My body burned hotter than a steam engine. Until I disentangled myself from the way Kendall messed me up, making me hard over stupid messages, then a coat was a nuisance.

I walked inside, the familiar scents flowing around me. The yeasty smell of beer saturated in fried bar food and peppered with the savory oregano odor of pizza. I went toward my normal spot at the far end of the bar, closest to the door, doing my usual sweep of the clientele.

Being a regular here was more out of convenience. The other regulars had been seeing me here for so long they ignored me, and the saloon-style bar didn't necessarily attract the business crowd I often ran in which kept the speculation and gossip about me to a minimum. This was more like a place I'd find back home in King's Creek, but way more private. The influx of guests staying for workshops and conferences helped keep the clientele fresh while being transient enough to maintain a nice level of anonymity.

There were indeed plenty of people. A conference must be in town. Normally, I'd meet a single woman close to my age as the rest of her group drifted off. We'd get to talking. Then I'd get invited up to her room. Most of the time, I left when we were done, before she got the wrong idea. Rarely, I stayed until morning. If I did, it was with the understanding that there'd be more sex, and maybe breakfast, but that would be the extent of it.

What a sad fucking routine.

No wonder Aiden hadn't considered any impact at all on Kate over what he did. The poor girl didn't know about the trust. I pondered my oldest son's relationship status as I took my seat.

Nodding to Rodrigo, I settled, knowing he'd bring me my regular. One Grand Marnier 1880 that he stocked just for me. I used to hate the stuff. DB drank it and served me a glass whether I asked for it or not. Since he did all the talking —boasting—harrumphing—I had sipped out of pure boredom. Now it was my thing.

My gaze skipped over the crowd, landing on a table of familiar thirty-somethings. Didn't I know them from work? One of the women shifted and I was able to see around the others.

Kendall.

As my gaze landed on her, she glanced up. Her brows lifted in surprise, and I didn't miss the panicked look she gave the rest of the table. They either hadn't seen me or didn't care.

But it was unusual to see my employees here. It was why I preferred it.

I schooled my own shocked expression into a half smile and dipped my head. Rodrigo saved me by sliding my drink in front of me.

"Busy night," he said before I even asked.

"Those are the best Fridays."

"Especially when you're the owner." He grinned and hustled to the other side to grab an order.

I tried to concentrate on anything but Kendall. I'd only caught a glimpse, but I knew she wore a wrap-around dress that probably made her legs look fantastic. If she had on those knee-high boots again, I would need a few extra minutes in the shower. Her ass landing in my arms was the visual that never failed to push me over the edge. Saved on water.

Awareness crawled all over me. Was she looking at me or everyone else?

A shadow appeared at my side. I looked over, ready to

greet Kendall, but a woman closer to my age slid onto the stool next to me. She smiled at me in a way that told me exactly what she wanted. "Is this seat taken?"

"No, ma'am."

I focused on my drink. Rodrigo came over to take her order, giving me a bemused head shake when the woman wasn't looking. I never had to troll the bar. The women came to me.

Except Kendall.

"You look familiar," she said.

I repressed my sigh. How rude would it be to leave my drink and go? I didn't want to toss it back and then hop behind the wheel. It was one glass, but if I was pulled over, I'd smell like a distillery.

Giving her a tight smile, I said, "I don't believe we've met."

Her grin widened and she swiveled toward me. "Well, let me change that. I'm—"

I was distracted from her introduction by a mass exodus of my employees. A couple of the women flicked their gazes toward me, rolled their lips together, and scurried out. The two guys nodded, their gazes darting away. If they were my kids, I'd think they were up to something.

I searched the table they'd been at. Where was Kendall? Had she left? Did she see me with this woman? I searched the bar for her.

"Is something wrong?" the woman asked.

"Looking for a friend."

"Funny, I was trying to do the same," she muttered and turned back to the bar.

There. A flash of honey-blond caught my eye. Kendall coming out of the hallway that led to the bathrooms and speeding toward her group—who had all left.

I watched as she stumbled to a stop, a frown on those pretty lips. I wanted to fire every one of them.

Ironic. This was why they had fraternization policies. All we had at King Oil was a *don't be stupid* policy if you dated someone within the company. And a transfer policy if you dated someone in your chain of command, but we only enforced it if there were issues. I'd been staunchly against implementing a separate fraternization policy. Our offices and work sites were in small towns in rural America. It was highly possible to meet your other half at work.

I had just never expected I'd be looking at someone who not only made me think about other halves again, but tempted me to violate the *don't be stupid* policy.

CHAPTER 15

endall

THOSE BASTARDS. Damn them all. Every. Single. One.

It'd taken a moment to dawn on me what happened. But as I stared at my empty table, acutely aware of Gentry sitting next to some attractive woman who looked more like the ones he'd been pictured with in the media, I realized I'd been played.

Gentry had a regular spot. And they all knew it. Just like they thought I'd slept with him.

It wasn't a coincidence that after he arrived, and after the woman sauntered toward him, they'd left me.

What if I hadn't gone to the bathroom?

But I had, and I'd ridden here with Dina from accounting. Who was gone.

I did one more frantic search of the bar, hoping my group proved me wrong, that people weren't as wicked as I assumed.

No luck.

But Gentry was witness to my humiliation. I could see enough out of the corner of my eye. He was watching the whole thing play out. And the woman was still next to him, her ass managing to look good even on a bar stool.

Okay. Game plan. I'd go over to the table and call for a ride. Maybe Brendell would be around. He might ask a lot of questions, since I hadn't called him to save me since my prom date puked all over the inside of his Toyota Corolla.

I chose to spare my pride and call a cab.

No one else was paying attention to me. They didn't know I'd been ditched.

I sat down and pulled up all my options to get a car to drive me away from this nightmare.

"Need a ride?"

My head jerked up almost as fast as a wave of lust crashed through my body. Gentry was standing over me. His hands in his pockets, his expression full of sympathy.

My stomach twisted, humiliation wringing out of it. He'd seen the whole thing.

"It seems I do." I looked past him to the woman. She was sipping a drink that looked like a sunrise. "I'm calling for a ride."

He tilted his head toward the door. "Come on. I'll take you back to your car."

He spoke softly, but his words carried over the din. I slumped my shoulders. "I don't want to intrude."

His brow furrowed. "On what?"

"Your night. You *know*." I glanced toward the woman again. She was speaking to the bartender, but he was focused on Gentry, curiosity evident in his gaze.

"Know what?" His lips twisted like he was fighting a smile.

I was tempted to smile, but the situation was too pathetic. "I don't want to cock block you."

"I believe that's your brother's specialty." I sputtered over my laugh and he grinned. "Come on. I came here to unwind, not sleep with anyone. I might've made small talk to keep from being rude, but that's all."

Right. His promise to his sons. A nice little topping to my mortification. I rose and put my coat on. "I'm parked at the office."

His gaze swept over my coat. Was he remembering our nights bundled together? Because I did. The kiss especially kept me up at night in my tiny, loud apartment.

I followed him out. He swaggered through the crowd as if he didn't see a single person. There was no side-stepping or excuse-mes. The crowd parted like he was the king of more than an oil company. He'd earned the crown in the logo.

What would that make me? I was tucked into my coat to hide from anyone else who'd seen me ditched. The jester? I'm sure my coworkers were having a nice laugh at my expense.

He held the door open for me, and I gladly let the wind slap me in the face. All my coworker's small talk and inviting me to sit with them at the break room. It was fake. I was transported back to high school. To when that prom date had only asked me out because he'd heard I was a virgin. And when it was clear I wasn't putting out, he'd proceeded to drink himself into a stupor. Times like that, Brendall was there for me without question, the same when he'd talked to me for an hour after I caught Darren cheating and then helped me find a lawyer.

That was why I put family first. I just hated the reminder that people sucked

"I'm sorry," Gentry said quietly as he led me toward his ride. I guessed it was the pickup at the end of the lot that looked like it could be out in a muddy field right about now, towing a tractor out of the muck. Or whatever ranchers did with pickups.

"It's not your fault. I should've known it was too good to be true. I was never the pinnacle of the social crowd. So, you come here often?" It was my lame attempt at humor, but mostly I wanted to redirect the conversation.

"I guess my secret's out." He opened the door for me and a waft of his scent crowded around me. Soap and a dash of sandalwood cologne. I could crawl in the back seat and go to sleep. It'd be even better if he got in there behind me. But I was passed over once already tonight, I didn't need for it to happen again.

I climbed in and sunk as far in the seat as possible. I looked so forward to tonight. To not going home right away to stare at four walls. To not fielding calls from Jen about her essay on *The Scarlett Letter* that's due on Monday. To not wondering if Gentry went back to his bar and picked up company.

That last part I would've done regardless.

"What's up for your weekend?" he asked as he pulled out of the lot.

"I was going to help my sister with an essay. I finally agreed to read it over once she finished it."

"Learned the hard way?"

"That she'd try to get me to write it? Yes." We shared a grin that those who'd raised like-minded teenagers could share.

This is what I missed. It wasn't how attracted I was to him, but how he got me. Parents who'd raised teens often didn't take me seriously when we talked about kids. Gentry did. "How about you?"

"Work. Are you surprised?"

I angled myself toward him as street lights flashed through the windows. "Don't you ever go home?"

He slid his gaze toward me, then back on the road. "I work all weekend and hope that Dawson calls and needs help. Helping on the ranch is all the time off I need."

"Why don't you offer?"

"It's his business."

He was a good dad. I know he blamed himself for so many things, but he had four independent sons who were all successful in their own right.

I should stare back out the window, but I wanted to keep looking at him and his strong profile, the way the lights flashed over his hair and face, making the silver flecks at his temples flicker. At the moment, I couldn't hate my coworkers for ditching me.

He pulled into the parking lot of King Oil. I always parked toward the end of the lot. There was my little gray car. All by itself. He parked next to it.

Gentry put the pickup in park. "Do you want to start it and let it warm up?"

It was time to go. In my cold car. To my empty apartment. There was no reason to delay the inevitable. "No, but thanks for the offer." I smiled, trying to keep the sadness from entering my eyes. Why couldn't we be together again? Why was being with him a bad idea?

Right. Because of everyone else.

"And thanks for the ride." With that, I climbed out of his pickup. After being in his vehicle with its heated seats, touch display, voice commands, and epic leg room, my car was going to make the night even more pathetic.

By the time I got around the box of the pickup, a door shut.

"Kendall." Gentry had gotten out.

His stricken expression prompted me to cover the ground between me and him. I looked up and into his dark eyes. My breath puffed out and exhaust swirled around us. "Yes?"

"I...I don't want this to be the end. Of us." He closed his mouth, his gaze traveling down to my boots, the same ones I'd been wearing the day we met. "And when you wear those boots... Damn." He bent and my dreams unfolded before my eyes. He was going to kiss me.

No, he was going to stop, remind me why this was a bad idea as if I didn't know and then I'd go home alone.

But he didn't. He kissed me.

Neither of us took it slow. I wanted to pick up exactly where we'd left off that day in Douglas. He deepened the kiss, his tongue plundering my mouth, tasting of fruity alcohol. I don't know what he had been drinking, but he made it taste exquisite.

"Gentry," I managed to take control of my own tongue. "I don't want this to be the end either."

"You don't have to go anywhere," he growled. "Unless it's with me."

I was about to ask where we should go when his mouth crashed against mine. He backed me up, only one of his arms around me. Being in his embrace again wiped out my good sense. I didn't care if it was early spring in Montana and that we were in the middle of the parking lot. But I was still grateful when the backdoor of his pickup swung open. I didn't wait for his invite. I scrambled inside to the wide back seat, uncaring of the fabric bunching under me.

He crowded inside, slamming the door shut behind him. The dome light faded, leaving us lit only by the parking lot lights. As he pressed me against the seat, I widened my legs, cradling him with my right leg propped against the driver's seat and my left leg pushing into the back door. His hard erection pressed into the perfect spot. It'd been too long since I'd been left hanging with no relief. I rocked against him, earning another groan.

We didn't take our time. He unwrapped me like I was his special gift on Christmas morning. My coat was off and my belt was losing the battle to hold together the top of my dress. Warm lips captured my nipple through the lacy material of my bra. I wanted to touch his skin so I fisted his shirt and pried it free of his waistband. Just shy of spreading my hands across his bare back, I had to give up as he gripped my hips in his big hands and boosted me higher onto the seat.

My breath hitched. He was lowering himself to the floor and lifting my leg until it stuck between the two front seats, opening me to him. The skirt had ridden up my thighs, but he yanked it up, lifting me enough to get it under my bottom.

Somewhere, my mind chimed in that it was a good thing King Oil didn't need security guards for the office building.

His eyes were boring into mine. "I've been dying to know what you taste like, Kendall."

A shiver traced through my body, but my brain still managed unwarranted honesty. "A sexually repressed twenty-eight-year-old?"

"I'll take care of that." He lowered his head.

My underwear was shoved out of the way and held to the side by his thumb. When he descended on me, my chest constricted. Then his tongue was on me, finding my clit as if the dome light came on and shone right on it. My head fell back and a long moan escaped.

This was nothing like getting myself off. It was nothing like being with my ex. Neither did it compare to any experience I'd ever had. They all paled compared to hot sex in a pickup with an older man who knew what the hell he was doing. The only word coursing through my mind was *finally*.

Gentry proved it with every stroke of his tongue.

His shoulders braced my thighs apart and he licked and sucked until I was panting and afraid I'd lose my mind if I didn't come. It was intoxicating.

I clutched the back of the seat with my one hand and held myself in place with my other on the headrest. If it wasn't so dark, I'd probably see that my knuckles were white. But my hips moved of their own accord and I didn't want to fall onto the floor.

My gasp escapes. "Yes. Yes. Y—"

He thrust a finger inside, and the word dissolved into a moan. My head thrashed. I wanted to hold on longer, but my body had never been mastered like this. He was in control, but not even he could prolong this orgasm.

A wave of ecstasy slammed into me. I jammed my hips into his mouth and rode the crest as long as I could. My walls clenched around his finger, and blazing heat washed over me as I shook against him.

He finally released me. "God, that was fucking amazing, Kendall."

I liked hearing him say my name. It seemed like he said it as often as he could, like he'd been unable to for too long.

He reared up and reached behind him. His wallet. A condom. My gaze went to his pants, where his erection pushed against his slacks. He flipped open his belt, then his fly, and there it was. Even that was the most masculine dick I'd ever seen. Long and thick and straining.

He rolled the condom on and propped a knee on the seat. His body covered mine. My legs were stuck where they were, but I let go of the seats and wrapped my arms around his neck.

He didn't fumble. He didn't hesitate. He was as serious about sex as he was about the rest of life, but he did pause only to ask, "Are you ready?"

"God, yes." If he waited any longer, I'd die a quick death.

Snaking an arm behind me and tugging me close, he coated himself by dragging his cock through my folds, then pushed inside in one steady, controlled move.

He filled me so completely that my body needed time to adjust.

The hard look in his eyes softened. "You feel even better than I imagined." He kicked his pelvis back and then pumped hard. "And I imagined it a lot."

So had I. My eyelids drifted shut. "More."

He gave it to me, claiming my mouth as he claimed me. It was just the right pace. Long, hard strokes at my core, and teasing my mouth with his tongue. The sensations were overwhelming. He was over me, in me, and claiming me.

Was this what we'd been missing for four days together?

I felt cheated.

"Kendall," he groaned. His thrusts came faster, and he held me in place, rocking the large pickup. I loved the flex of his back muscles as he pumped.

I kissed my way down his chin, along his neck, stopping at the base of his neck. The salt of his flesh mingled with the flavor of me, stoking the brush fire that hadn't died down after my first orgasm.

I never came twice this quickly. Before, it was always work. Something that had to be planned because it was possible, but it took a lot of effort.

My second orgasm tonight was going to hit. And when he let me go to brace his arms against the seats and slam into me, I careened over the edge.

My hands twisted in his shirt as I came, my head smacking the window and my body shuddering. He went rigid, only his hips swinging. We climaxed together. Another thing that had always been impossible. But not with him.

He sagged, his eyes closed and his head hanging, but he

didn't collapse on me. "I…fuck, Kendall. That was…" His eyelids flipped open, the heat in them warming me down to my toes. "I don't care if you come to my place, or I go to yours, but I want to spend the weekend so buried in you that I won't know when Monday hits. And I want you to keep these fucking boots on."

entry

My life before these last two weeks hadn't seemed so dreary and empty until that episode with Kendall in the back of the truck. I'd taken a detour after our quickie to adjust the footage of the security cameras and erase that view of us disappearing into my vehicle, but then I'd brought her home.

We managed to meet up in the evenings when I wasn't traveling, and this Friday night, she brought me home. I was sprawled across her discount couch, my dick in her mouth, and she was sucking on me like I'd dipped it in sugar. Yeah, my life before Kendall had been day-old muffins. Now it was fresh baked, full of sweetness—and heart-stopping blowjobs.

My head lolled back, but only momentarily. Tonight, it didn't seem to matter how often I'd had this done, or by how many, this was it. The most erotic of them all, and I didn't want to miss the show.

Kendall with her bare ass pushed out, her waist tucked in. Her hair draped over my pelvis and stomach, and her eyes closed, occasionally opening to connect with me. My own personal goddess.

I was certain that every sound we made went straight through her walls to the neighbors. I was used to doing it in hotel rooms, and even the walk of no-shame the next morning, but this seemed infinitely more intimate.

I had to bite back a loud groan. I don't know what she just did with her tongue, but my hips rocketed off the couch, momentarily choking her. "Shit, sorry. But do it again."

There was a smile in her eyes, before her tongue rimmed the top of my cock and she sucked me back in. I buried my hands in her hair and tried to recite the alphabet backward to keep from embarrassing myself. I usually outlasted a woman, until I took over out of pity. But not with Kendall.

"I'm going to come. If you don't want—"

She tightened her hold on the base of my shaft and did that thing with her tongue, the swirling lick that would make me her servant forever, and I was lost. Lightning shot down my spine, my balls drawing up, and I climaxed right into her mouth. When she was done, she released me with a pop and gave me a lazy smile.

I couldn't move. My glistening dick lay on my stomach, and my legs were limp. Summoning enough energy to draw her up next to me, I held her tight and covered us with the throw blanket from the back of the couch, her plush one with the kitties all over it.

Her hair was adorably rumpled, but in the sexiest way. Like usual, if she wore makeup I couldn't tell. Her cheeks were flushed and her eyes bright, but her body was snug against mine.

The post-coital glow probably wasn't the time to make sweeping declarations, but I couldn't go without saying something. This thing with Kendall? It wasn't superficial. I was a businessman. I was also a rancher. Both required me to read the conditions before I acted, and I'd learned to listen to my intuition. "I haven't felt this way about anyone, Kendall. Not in a long time." Not ever.

She blinked at me, her gaze growing guarded. "What do you mean?"

"I want to take it to the next level. You deserve better than sneaking around."

She'd told me that the Monday after she was ditched at the bar, she ignored all her coworkers and took her break and lunch in her office, arriving early and leaving late to avoid them. It killed me not to act on her behalf, but she insisted it'd make it worse.

Turning toward me, her bare breasts rubbing against my chest. Nope, I didn't want to walk away from those. "I want to be with you. I like you, Gentry. I feel like I've found…" Her teeth worried her lower puffy lip. "I feel like I've found *you*. But it seems like the odds are stacked against us with work and your kids."

"I know." This is what I'd missed my whole life. Sarah and I had built a great life together, but after our first round of teenage hormone-driven sex, it was nothing but a lot of responsible decisions interwoven to create a foundation for our family. We'd been compatible, right down to our chemistry, but we'd been weighed down by everyone else's expectations. Kendall already had that; I didn't want to add to it.

"So, now what?" she asked.

A faint buzzing interrupted my suggestion of a real date. In public. In Billings. I hated to pull away, but my phone was in my pants at my feet.

"Go ahead." She reached over me and I took the opportunity to caress her ass, enjoying the slope and the slide of her soft skin. She brandished my phone and snuggled back in. "You don't have to apologize to me for working all the time."

Now that was something I never heard.

I looked the screen. Dawson. It was almost midnight. My fatherly instincts reared up. "What's going on?"

Wind rushed over the line. "Do you have big plans this weekend? Kiernan helped pull a calf in the dark and broke his damn ankle."

Kiernan was one of the hired hands. "Is he all right?"

Dawson let out a frustrated snort. "It was all I could do to get him to go to the hospital. He kept insisting it was only a sprain even while his foot was hanging funny. He's out for weeks, and I've got calves dropping like midnight rain."

I looked down at Kendall. Her luminous eyes were serious. She'd heard it all. Her expression softened. She nodded and mouthed *go*.

We were just talking about going to the next level. It was an important conversation, and I didn't want to up and leave.

"Yeah, but I might have company."

What possessed me to ask Kendall to go back to my hometown and stay with my son?

All I knew was that after expecting a weekend enjoying her company and her body, bringing her along had seemed like a good idea. But each mile closer to King's Creek, where I would be recognized in gas stations and at red lights, I wasn't sure. She'd get a lot of attention, and I couldn't promise it'd be good.

I wasn't even sure she'd agree to come with, but she was tucked into the passenger seat. The glow of King's Creek was up ahead, but I turned off the highway onto the dirt roads that led to my family's ranch.

Dawson hadn't asked who I'd bring. He probably thought I'd coerce Aiden into coming out. I should've. The kid could use a break, even if it was slogging through the muck to check on calves and their mamas.

It was barely past ten in the morning. We'd gotten an early start, eating breakfast on the road. Kendall had packed a bag, and I swung by my house, wondering what she'd think about my old home in King's Creek.

"You sure he won't mind I'm tagging along?" she asked.

"Out of all my sons, Dawson's the most easygoing. About me anyway." If we were heading to Denver to face Beckett, I would've spared her. Aiden, I wasn't sure. I don't think he suspected I was seeing someone, and he probably wouldn't believe it was an unofficially committed relationship. Xander didn't talk to me enough for me to know whether he'd be upset that I was bringing a woman into their childhood home, one who was their age, not mine.

"He's easygoing about you and women, you mean?"

"I've never brought anyone home since I saw how badly it affected Beckett. I'd bring dates to work functions where a plus one was expected. To restaurant or gallery openings, but never to my house in Billings, or to King's Creek once I moved."

Her eyes reflected her worry, but I could still see the pleasure shining through them. She liked my confession.

She was special, and I wanted her to know.

We were quiet the rest of the way. As my house—Dawson's house—came into view, I divided my attention between the road and her. In the daylight, the magnitude of our land was clear. Pastures sweeping left and right over the rolling hills as far as the eye could see. Cows dotted the land and snow was only visible where it had piled the highest over the winter, the rest had melted. Three long barns were pinwheeled out, surrounded by fencing and more cows.

Tractors were parked in front of the large shop doors or next to the buildings.

"Whoa," Kendall breathed, staring at the log structure that was as big as a skiing lodge. Large picture windows reflected the sun and the field. The house was the closest thing to a legacy that I had.

"Sarah and I built it when the boys were little." Again, I marveled over how easy it was to talk to her about my late wife. "It's still our hub. The place might be Dawson's, but if my boys are going to get together, it's here."

"It's beautiful." The terrain wasn't much different than Billings, but with the lack of industry and a clearer view of the Yellowstone River valley, it painted a prettier picture. She turned to me, her eyes wide. "These are the framed photographs in your office."

"Sarah loved photography. Not as much as ranching, but she could do both."

"The pictures in your office and Aiden's are hers?"

I nodded. "All over. You'll see them in the house too."

"Wow, that's solid branding."

I chuckled.

"Seriously, I could use some of her photos in our brochures."

Memories welled up, tugging at my heart. We'd had a good life. "She had that idea once. Her mom didn't go for it, wanted it to be all about industry and growth."

"Take it back to the beginning. If she has some of North Dakota, I could start there. I'm the new marketing professional for that region, you know?"

The corner of my mouth lifted. "I think I heard about that."

Dawson sauntered out of the front door, a mug in his hand and his brown hair mussed like he had just rolled out of bed. He'd have his hat on if he was heading out. Taking a sip, my son narrowed his eyes on the pickup as I swung by the front to park on the side with the garage. He froze when he saw my passenger, only his mouth dropped open.

"You're not kidding you don't bring anyone home," Kendall murmured.

"He looked a little surprised, didn't he?"

I parked and jogged around to her side to help her out. Drifts of snow crowded the house and the sides of the driveway where it had been pushed off the main areas. It was a spring morning and the ground alternated between thin ice from melt-off and patches of mud.

Once her feet hit the pavement, her gaze tracked me from head to toe. "I can't get over…you."

I was wearing worn jeans and a plaid flannel with my tan Carhartt coat over it. My Oxford loafers had been traded for my favorite pair of cowboy boots. They were ragged, most of their color faded to a light brown, but they were comfortable and I'd been wearing them for years. "Suits don't hold up well to amniotic fluid and manure."

She grinned and accepted my elbow. I led her around the house instead of going through the garage. Dawson was at the edge of the porch, leaning over it, with his cup held loosely in his hands.

"Morning," he said, his eyes drifting from me to Kendall.

"Dawson." I was about to say *you look like hell*, but this was already awkward. "Late night?"

His gaze shifted to the pasture closest to the calving barn. "Late night and early morning. I just made it back to the house for some breakfast."

"How's Kiernan?"

"Planted on his ass, I hope." Dawson's trademark lazy grin reminded me so much of his mother. "But still trying to convince me to put him back to work." He took a long sip. "Who's your friend?"

"Kendall Brinkley, my, uh...we're seeing each other."

Dawson's brows knit together. "Like, you're seeing her more than once?" He gave her a sheepish grin. "No offense, ma'am."

She smiled. "None taken. I understand I'm an oddity."

Dawson straightened, his gaze full of approval. "And you're okay with that? Huh."

It was best to get it all out there. "Your Grams is going to be pissed. Beckett's going to think she's a gold digger, but she's the real deal. I couldn't stay away."

"And he tried," Kendall added.

"Sounds like a helluva story," Dawson drawled. "Why don't you tell me over breakfast."

 endall

DAWSON WAS A RIOT. And considerate. Gentry told him the whole story over pancakes Dawson refused to let me help make. And they were the best pancakes I'd ever tasted.

He also assured me that Beck wouldn't hunt me down and shoo me away from Gentry. Apparently, Beck didn't come home often.

I had the house to myself. Dawson and Gentry had gone out to the barn. A pickup pulled in and parked closer to one of the long barns. That must be one of the guys that worked for Dawson coming back from lunch. Hopefully not the one with the broken ankle.

I didn't know much about calving or what it required, but Dawson had looked haggard. There was a clear resemblance to Gentry, but he moved differently than his oldest brother. Aiden prowled like his father. Deliberate, determined strides.

Dawson flowed, his movements easy and relaxed. He had a devil-may-care air about him. It might be easy to write him off as not as intelligent as Aiden, but his eyes were clear, his gaze keen. What were the other brothers like?

I pegged Beck as similar to Aiden. Tightly controlled. As I let Gentry's computer fire up, I drifted through the house, looking at pictures. Xander had an easy smile like Dawson.

What would he think about me? Dawson seemed open-minded. The fact that Gentry had brought me home was enough for him. I believed Gentry when he said I was the first, but Dawson would've clinched it.

Were things between Gentry and I indeed that serious? I hadn't felt this way about Darren in the beginning. I'd been excited. Relieved mostly. I found a guy who'd stick around. He'd be my excuse to distance myself from my family. But it turned out that wasn't what I wanted.

I guess that wasn't fair to him.

But with Gentry, I just wanted to be with him. It wasn't about what he could do for me, and on his side, it wasn't about what I could do for him. I liked talking to him. I thought the work he did was fascinating, and I was crazy attracted to him. We were both family-centric.

I hadn't been this excited about a guy since...ever. And nervous. The nerves were going to kill me. My gaze kept sliding to the door. How often did Emilia stop by? She lived in Billings, but King's Creek was only a few hours east, not far from the North Dakota border.

If she heard I was here, would she hunt me down?

I was closer to Williston than I'd ever be for my job. Only today, I wasn't doing my normal job. I got to dig into Gentry's inbox and summarize his messages and streamline his priorities. Getting this much insight into his world was a gift I didn't take lightly. I loved marketing, but I mostly picked it because I could get jobs anywhere in the world. Only I had stayed in Billings.

But first, I had to check on Jen and that essay. It was due on Monday, and even though she'd had weeks to write it, I doubted she'd even begun.

I slid in front of Gentry's computer, dialed her, and put it on speaker.

She answered with, "I'm not done reading the book. Can you give me an hour?"

Normally, I wouldn't have called. I would've just gone over and she wouldn't have been ready and there I'd be, probably starting laundry or something. "Here's the thing, Jen. I had to go out of town for work." And she was supposed to have written the essay by now.

"What?" I could picture her in her oversized sweatshirt with her hair in a messy bun. "You never go out of town for work. You never go out of town, period."

My voice raised a couple of octaves. "Well, it's a new job."

"You're lying."

"Am not." She was over ten years younger than me, but we dissolved into the most juvenile arguments.

"Who is he?" And she was stubborn.

"Jen."

"Ken."

I sighed. Someone so young shouldn't be such a good lie detector. But she'd been younger than the others when she figured out Santa was me. Mom and Dad bought some clothes that didn't fit anyone and I sorted and wrapped them, often staying over on Christmas Eve with Darren. And I'd rush over before work in the morning to play Tooth Fairy because Mom and Dad opened the restaurant each morning and stayed through the breakfast rush before they went to the thrift store. Jen had spotted the pattern way sooner.

"Maybe I ran off with Darren. We might be trying to reconcile."

"Ooh, so what I'm hearing is that you don't think people will approve. Now I gotta know who he is."

"How do you— Never mind. If you think you know all this, you can figure out the essay."

"I get real people," she said dryly. "I don't get fictional women written by some guy hundreds of years ago."

"It was like a hundred and fifty years ago."

"We should make Darren wear a red A."

I started laughing. It was both easier and harder to keep helping my family out as they got older. They were turning into fun people. "I'm still in Montana. Happy?"

"Nope. Where?"

She was sharp. If I told her where, she'd guess. But then I did work for the company. "King's Creek."

Her gasp echoed through the house. I pulled up Gentry's endless inbox, cringing that she was going to guess at any moment. There was no good reason not to tell her. But I didn't.

Gentry's family would know before the day was done. We hadn't decided to officially go public. We'd just decided not to hide and let everyone figure it out, then deal with the fallout later. It wasn't stated in so many words, but understood. I'd made it to King's Creek. How many hurdles did I have to face in one day?

"King's Creek," she screeched. "That's where the oil Kings are from."

"King Oil. My new employer."

"Doesn't one of them work there? Which one, Kendall?"

"Gentry King runs the company with his oldest son." I went for it. My cheeks burned. "The son is married."

"No way, you went straight to the top. *Nice.*"

I told her what happened. The story poured out and I

realized that I'd been doing nothing but work and serving my siblings. I'd gone through my divorce alone even though my brothers and sisters constantly checked in—and told me that Darren was a bad idea in the first place.

But my only other option had been to move back home. Then I'd be sister-mom.

"Aw, Kendall. That's really sweet. Hold on, let me look up a picture of him."

I waited, my stomach twisting. Why was my family's opinion of Gentry so important? I never cared that they thought Darren was a dud.

"Well," she said. "He's younger than Dad."

"Jen."

"What? You go from that hold-my-beer guy after Darren to the King CEO? I'm impressed."

I poured sarcasm into my "Thanks."

"No, really. He's… Wow. He has four kids. Kendall. Ohmigosh, they're your age."

"Yup. Look, can you not tell anyone? It's really new and we want to gradually come out since we work together."

"Like any of my friends would care. Mom and Dad would have to be home for me to tell them. But, I mean, he's a lot older than you. What if he doesn't want kids? All his are grown."

"It's new, Jen." We had so many things to get past that kids weren't even on the radar and I had my own feelings about them. "You got it out of me, okay? Now go read your book and call me later if the essay trips you up."

"Got it."

She disconnected. Awareness prickled over my back. I closed my eyes. Who heard the conversation?

I opened them and looked toward a hallway that I hadn't been down. But since it was on the same side of the house as the garage, there must be another entrance.

Gentry was leaning against the wall, his expression grim. His hand was hooked in a loop of his jeans and his bulky coat did nothing to hide how in shape he was. "I came to warn you that Aiden's coming to help this weekend. He's bringing Kate. They'll be here in a little bit."

"Okay." If things went south, I wouldn't really see Aiden that much at the office. Gentry's troubled gaze stayed on me. "What's wrong?"

He pressed his lips together. "What your sister said." Walking to me, his gait was changed with his boots, exaggerated the cowboy swagger that was usually subtle in his shiny shoes. He pulled out the chair to my right and took a seat. "She's not wrong about me and kids. Once it was clear that I wasn't looking to settle down and that if I did, the woman would most likely be my age and over the family raising part of her life, I got a vasectomy. I know this thing between you and I just started, but you should know. And I wouldn't blame you if you moved on."

Oh. This thing between us did just start, but I'd been craving it my whole adult life. A stable guy. A partner. Not another responsibility. "Gentry, I don't want to have kids."

His brows shot up and he cocked his head. "You don't? But…"

"But I'm a young woman of child-bearing age and I should, right? I know. Except I was tucking Brendell in when I was five and he was three. I did most of the nighttime bottles for Jen and the twins because Mom and Dad had to work in the morning and they made mistakes with the books if they didn't get rest. I was old enough to understand how overwhelmed they were. I've changed more diapers than I care to remember. I've taken them to get their vaccinations, sat in on parent-teacher conferences, and bought them jockstraps and sports bras."

His expression darkened the more I talked. "That's a lot for a kid."

"Gentry, I'm still doing it. I called Jen because she needs help with her homework. And you know what? I should be wrapped up in bitterness, but I'm not. They drive me crazy and I love my family. I also helped raise them and I have no regrets, but I'm ready to live *my* life."

"You might change your mind when you're older," he murmured.

I let out a long exhale. "I might, but I might not. By then I'll have nieces and nephews to dote on and you'll have grandbabies." His eyes warmed at the idea of grandkids. God, that was sexy too. I dreamed of the day I could spoil a kid and send it on its way home. "I want to skip the step of having kids and go right to the grandparent stage."

"It's not just kids. I'm at the age where I'm thinking about my parents' health issues and what they mean for me."

"And I'm a woman and have been told by media my whole life that I'm eating wrong and need to lose weight. It's nothing new, Gentry."

He leaned in on his elbows and took my hands. His fingers stroked the top of my hands. "I feel like we skipped the beginning of dating and went right for the serious stuff."

"I feel like we're too old for the bullshit."

His soft chuckle draped around me like a warm blanket. "Ironically, I have Emilia to thank for some of the best things in my life. I can't believe she's the reason I met you."

"Well, I'm in it just for the money, you know." I squeezed his hands. I can't believe I could joke like this with him.

"If you were, you'd want a baby to seal the deal. Isn't that what the movies say?"

"Gentry King, you don't watch movies."

He grinned. "Not really." His smile faded. "But if we're in this for long-term, we should talk. About stuff."

He knew everything there was about me and what I wanted for my future. "Let's just enjoy being together and not completely pass over all the new beginning stages."

"I guess one heavy talk is enough for our first date."

"Technically, we haven't gone on a date."

He leaned forward, releasing my hand to cup my chin. His scent surrounded me as we kissed. Crisp fresh air and laundry detergent. These were probably the only items he didn't get dry cleaned.

Releasing me he rose, and subtly adjusted himself. "Tonight. There's a steakhouse in town that serves only King beef."

"It's a date, Mr. King."

He started back to the hallway and gestured to the computer. "It's the weekend. You don't have to work. You don't ever have to do any of my work."

"How am I going to get state secrets and overthrow your company if I don't?"

Those laugh lines I found so sexy appeared. "You'd need to target Emilia for that. You won't find anything in Mrs. Chan's weekly update of marketing efforts."

"I like this. It makes me feel like…" I chewed on my lower lip. I'd never said this out loud. "It makes me feel like I did more with my life than I really have."

Compassion warmed his eyes. "Kendall, you can do anything you want to."

"Thanks." But I stayed in Billings to help my family and I'd do it again.

The front door opened and we both swung our heads around to see who was entering. My heart pounded.

Aiden held the door for a woman with soft brown hair and a pleasant smile. That must be Kate. He came in after her, speaking low. Kate nodded, but spotted us and stopped. Her smile widened.

"Hello."

Aiden pulled to a stop behind her, his hand hovering behind her back. From my angle, he didn't appear to be touching her, but the move was proprietary nonetheless. Kate's expression was delighted, but Aiden's *you have some explaining to do* look was aimed at his dad.

This weekend was going to be interesting.

entry

"I'm TAKING her to Hogan's tonight." I rode a horse next to Dawson. My bay, King's Gold, was steady under me. He knew the route through the pastures and as long as another horse was out with him, he wouldn't keep veering toward the barn.

Dawson rode Beckett's horse, Black Gold, because he liked to exercise all of them, but mostly because he needed a sanity break away from pregnant cows. Aiden was even with us. He was a workaholic, but it didn't take much to get him to trade his car for a horse. I'd rather see him take his wife on vacation, but this was at least out of the office.

"You're going to get everyone talking," Dawson warned.

"They'll talk anyway. And no one knows who she is here. It's probably safer to start here than Billings."

Dawson peered at me from under the brim of his cowboy

hat. "Start? Aren't you two going steady, or whatever the kids call it these days?"

Aiden was quiet on Gold Mine, looking more relaxed than I'd seen him in months, but he wasn't missing a moment of the exchange. "Yeah, Dad. What's going on? Last you told me you weren't going to pursue her."

"It just...happened." Thanks to my employees that I had wanted to fire but now I wanted to reward with bonuses. They'd planned it. I didn't know if they intended to get her in trouble, or me, but it wasn't like I could go interrogating them. "I don't regret it. She's different."

Dawson snorted. "I'll say. She's younger than anyone you've ever been with."

My jaw tightened. "Is that a problem?"

"It's weird, but I can get over it," Aiden answered. "To Beck it will be though."

"You told him."

Aiden slid his gaze over. "Yes. And I left a message for Xander."

"You guys are worse than the church ladies."

Aiden shrugged, unrepentant. "You've never brought anyone home. And the storm, Grams, and the trust, and her age—it's a big deal."

The reminder of Emilia was colder than the wind at my back. At least the wind had a touch of warmth and carried the promise of summer. Emilia wasn't as optimistic. She wouldn't like the news that I was seeing Kendall. It'd wipe out what I told her about Douglas, mostly truth or not. "No, your grams isn't going to like it."

Aiden's gaze turned speculative. "What she's not going to like is how you're letting her help with inner office stuff. Only family gets in the inner office."

"She should let us hire someone. Both you and I need an assistant."

"Take it to the board." Aiden's tone was flat. We had each brought the issue to the board, but Emilia had kept control for a reason.

Dawson *tsked*. "Grams needs to move to Arizona and take up golfing."

I nodded, easing King's Gold around a pile of snow. We didn't need to be out this far. Dawson had the cows in the winter pastures closer to the barn, but as the sun rose higher, it beat the chill back. The space helped me think, kept me from wondering how Kendall and Kate were getting along and hoping they loved each other. Preventing me from thinking about Kendall's declaration and wondering if she meant it.

She was divorced. Didn't want kids. Loved working. And she was wrapped in an adorable package that looked like she should be driving a van load of kids to soccer practice and then heading home and baking cookies.

I'd been married to that woman. Sarah had also been industrious, smart, and ambitious. I guess I had a type.

"I'd better head back." Dawson angled Black Gold in an arc to swing around to the barn. The rest of our horses followed.

"Tucker brought his daughter." Dawson's other employee had pulled up when I went to speak to Kendall. "I hear the girl is a real calf whisperer."

"She loves bottle feeding and has a good intuition about it. I'd hire her if she wasn't only thirteen." He grinned. "So, I set up an account. Each calf she bottle feeds, she gets a deposit. Only her parents know."

"And she thinks she's working for free." Aiden's eyes twinkled. "A future rancher right there."

"Tucker said that's her plan." Dawson shrugged. "I've been thinking about putting away enough that she can buy out the Cartwright's when she's eighteen."

"We can dream, right," Aiden said.

I rode in silence. The Cartwright land bordering ours was my family land, cheated away from my parents in a stupid poker game when my dad was Aiden's age. Danny was going to drink himself to death and there was no way his daughter Bristol could resurrect the mess her father had made of it. The pastures needed time and TLC, and the ranch needed all new buildings and equipment. Bristol might have all the time in the world to run the ranch, but not the money.

Was that what Sarah had been thinking when she set up the trusts? She'd bonded with Bristol. The girl would run over to play with the boys who usually ignored her then she'd find refuge in Sarah's office, or in the kitchen learning to cook.

I hadn't thought about the Cartwright drama much since Sarah had died. My income from the oil company kept the ranch going financially, and I had much more flexibility hiring people to work cattle than I did with an assistant.

Then Aiden had been approaching twenty-nine and our lawyer had met with me and Emilia.

Emilia doubled down on the oil company like she was afraid it'd get snatched away from her like she'd done to the Cartwrights with their mineral rights.

The Cartwrights took our land, but the Boyds took their oil rights. It seemed they got the raw end of the deal eventually.

But the whole scenario had made Emilia a ruthless businesswoman who fiercely protected what she thought was hers. As if she expected her lifelong friend to roll over and let the Boyds take what they wanted from the land and then go out for lunch later. With no friends, Emilia only trusted family. I'd become family when I married Sarah and had four sons. Emilia had looked the other way when it came to my indiscretions because I was one of the few she trusted. I was still family.

She wasn't going to take Kendall digging into company business very well. She would issue one of the ultimatums she was so fond of, and I was going to have to make a decision.

~

KENDALL SIGHED AND SAT BACK. "That was really good. Like, the best steak I've ever had."

Glassware tinkled around us. Hogan's was a casual country restaurant with high-end food. Wood beams arched over us and pictures of horses and cattle lined the walls. They served quality cut tender meat, expertly seasoned, that could rival any Michelin restaurant, but with a side of fries and ranch dressing. When I traveled for work and was served dry chicken breast over rice pilaf with seasonal vegetables, I missed Hogan's.

She took a sip of her ice water. "That came from the ranch?"

"Dawson has direct arrangements with a few businesses. He also supplies the butcher shop downtown."

"You must be so proud."

"I am." Not many of my dates knew enough about my kids to ask questions, and if they did it wasn't in the fond way Kendall did. I was more than a CEO who happened to have grown kids. To her, I was Gentry, a father and a businessman. I had feelings. "How'd Jen's essay go?"

Kendall rolled her eyes. "She sent it to me. I think she dictated it in like five minutes. It was riddled with typos and had no punctuation. I told her to clean it up and send it back."

"She was hoping you'd take care of it? What's the story with your parents?"

Her smile dissolved. "They're just *so busy*. It's become their story. First the thrift shop they opened had required a lot of work, but wasn't the payoff they hoped for. So they opened a restaurant to keep the family afloat. Ironically, they went into business for themselves so they had the flexibility for us kids. But I get it. Raising six kids is expensive and takes a lot of time, and they're afraid of being gone if something goes wrong at the store or diner. They're the businesses that help support us, and they're the businesses that will help secure their eventual retirement."

"You did well with your brothers and sisters."

Her smile was serene and a blush tinted her cheeks. "Thanks."

Our date was wrapping up, and I wanted nothing more than to take her home and get back between those curvy thighs and hear the way she said my name when she came. But we were staying in Xander's old room that had been converted to a guest room like the other bedrooms. I might've had dalliances under the roof when the house was still mine, but I wouldn't do it when it was my son's place.

Then again, we hadn't had a problem in the back seat of my pickup, and it was parked out in the lot. I knew a lot of quiet places where no one would bother us.

"Well, isn't this a surprise."

My libido was crushed by Emilia's voice.

"Emilia." I rose to pull out one of the empty chairs at our four-seater table. She probably knew the second I had arrived in King's Creek. Between my own kids and the ranch hands and idle town gossip, I'm sure it hadn't taken long for her to hear I wasn't alone.

Since Emilia knew I wouldn't bring just anyone back to King's Creek, she'd come to see for herself.

She floated down into the chair, her back rigid, and not a single hair of her silver bob out of place. "I see Beck was right. You and Ms. Brinkley."

I gave Kendall a reassuring smile. She'd gone ramrod straight, her face draining of color. "Yes, we've started seeing each other. Would you like a drink?"

"And the bullshit about moving that position? It was only so you could get laid?" She leaned closer, her voice low and tight. "I thought you'd be the last one to fuck with my company like this."

Anger simmered in my veins. I turned, dropping my voice just as low. "This isn't about Kendall's job performance or my sex life. When have I ever given you reason to doubt my commitment to the company?"

She relaxed, but only slightly. "I'd have less of a reason if you were concerned at all about Beck gaining access to his trust."

"My role as his father surpasses money."

"Then I worry that your role as lover will surpass good sense." Emilia's gaze flicked over to Kendall. "No offense, dear, but if you're at work on Monday, Gentry and I are going to have a long talk about his future at King Oil."

I recoiled, my vision tunneling in like I was scoping out the enemy. She not only threatened my job, but Kendall's? This was going too far.

"Ms. Boyd..." Kendall's voice shook.

"That's the last I have to say to you." Emilia put her back toward Kendall. "I'm not just doing this about the company. I'm looking out for your relationship with your son. Beck was in quite a state when he called."

"Beck knows nothing about this." My son hardly came to see me anymore. He thought my dick ruled my life and that I chose it over him.

"He knows enough." Emilia stood, thumping her chair in with her knee, and left. "I'll be in the office on Monday."

I ground my teeth together and met Kendall's wide gaze. "I'll deal with her."

"Maybe she's right." She might as well have gut punched me. Kendall shook her head, her eyes shining. "If the big problem with us is me at the company, then it's best I leave. If she found out I was directly helping you…"

"You can't quit your job because she threatened you."

"I'm quitting my job because I don't need this drama. Between Ms. Boyd and my coworkers, I need to go somewhere where my presence doesn't alienate others. And Beck would take us more seriously if I wasn't at King Oil."

"I will deal with both Emilia and Beck."

"Gentry, I didn't apply at King Oil. You got the job for me. I took it because I was desperate, and I like it, but…" She lifted a shoulder. "It's not just Ms. Boyd. I liked working directly with you. I have some money saved and I can look for executive assistant positions—that aren't with King Oil."

I considered her. She'd taken the job because she felt backed into a corner? What else had I expected? That she'd jumped on it to be close to me? "It's your decision, Kendall, but I want you to make it with *you* in mind, not with what everyone else wants in mind."

She worried her lower lip. "I'm going to make lemonade out of Emilia's lemons."

I didn't say anything. She'd been unhappy at the job since her coworkers tricked her, and she wanted to move on and move up. I wasn't going to be the one to stifle her.

 endall

IF APPLYING for jobs was a job, I wouldn't have to worry about money.

I was stretched out on my living room floor, combing through job openings, my laptop only taking five minutes to load each site. I should go buy a new one, but I'd rather secure an income before I went spending hundreds of dollars.

There was a knock on the door.

"Yo, Kennie. It's me."

What was Brendell doing here on a Tuesday? I'd taken all last week to feel sorry for myself and alternate between being grateful that I didn't have to face my spiteful coworkers anymore, and rage that Emilia Boyd could dictate my future and her son-in-law's like that. Seeing underneath the problem didn't help. Ms. Boyd had major control issues. Gentry and her grandsons weren't exempt because they were her family. Gentry was the son she never had, and he shouldered the brunt of the company, the one she and her husband had built from the ground up. Without Gentry she might lose it all. So she was a little territorial.

Just because I understood didn't make it right.

So, yeah. I'd left the job like a naughty puppy with my tail tucked between my legs. Then I'd cried. And had ice cream and rejoiced. Then went for a walk every day because the sun was out and the excess of dairy gave me a stomach ache. I had to fit into my interview clothing and after the food fest in King's Creek, I wasn't sure that'd happen.

"Just a minute." I popped off the floor and ran to the door. Swinging it open, I faced my brother. His hair was a darker blond than mine, and he was several inches taller. Concern brewed in his eyes. "What's up?"

He stalked in without waiting to be invited. "Mom and Dad. They want to know how you're doing and if you're moving back home."

"But I paid for a year here." Having a guaranteed roof over my head had made the decision to leave King Oil easier.

"We heard you lost your job again."

"How—"

"Jen saw you out walking in the middle of the day. It's not like you've been there long enough to get a week off."

I knew I should've gone the other direction and varied my route. "So, you assumed I lost my job?"

He shrugged. "Dating the boss means he doesn't lose his job when you two break up."

"We didn't break up." And he thought Gentry would fire me if we did? But then none of my family had met him. "It was a conflict of interest."

"And he's at work in his big office?"

"It's a family company. I didn't like the position anyway."

That was a little lie. I'd liked working and my big office was a nice bonus.

"Then why'd you take it?"

"Money. I think we've used up fifteen of your twenty questions. What'd you stop by for?"

"Call Mom and Dad. They're worried."

And that's why I was never too hard on them. They gave up everything for their kids—including time. Mom might be at the diner now, but she'd taken a moment to get Brendell to come check on me. "I'll give them a call."

He pinned me with a hard look. "You can also say no once in a while. Wendell will survive if you don't answer the phone."

It was an old argument. When Brendell moved out, he set firm boundaries. When he got married, he made even stricter ones. But I'd been there for every major sibling milestone. I wasn't going to walk away now. So I changed the subject. "Are you going to Wendell and Lenny's game?"

"When I get off work, I'll swing by."

I had wanted to ask Gentry, but without me helping him, he was back to being swamped.

God, that sounded pathetic. Was I only helping him so I could be around him?

No, I really enjoyed that work. Nothing against marketing. I was adequate at it, but it didn't come together like the full package of the company. It was just one facet. I loved having my hands sunk into everything. I was CEO material without the direct personality and the experience or education. Go me.

Gentry hadn't cut me off as soon as I logged out of his email. He'd stopped by every night after work, or I went to his place for supper. We'd spent part of last weekend together in bed.

"Ren's even coming home for it," Brendell added.

I laughed. "She's coming home for some other reason and just happens to be able to go to the game."

"You should take lessons." He looked around the tiny apartment. "You doing okay?"

"Yeah, why?"

"You don't usually, you know, go out for walks."

"I do, too." Not really. But last week I walked five days in a row. Maybe a mile one day, three the next. But there'd been nothing else to do and going back home meant I had to think about what I wanted to be when I grew up.

And that I was the mistress of a tycoon.

"All right." The skepticism was heavy in his eyes. "See you tonight then."

Once I was alone again, I faced the computer. My phone was lying next to it. Its screen flashed on then went black. I had a message.

Crossing the twenty feet to my phone didn't convince me that I had answered Brendell honestly. Was I all right?

The message was from Gentry. *Late meeting tonight. Won't be able to meet for supper.*

I stared at it for a minute before I sent a reply. *The twins have a game. You can stop by when you're done. They usually play until eight or later.*

He probably wouldn't get done in time. That's what I told myself. Because the last week felt like we'd gone back into hiding. I'd met his family and it blew up in our faces. I doubted he'd want to go out of his way to meet mine.

I CLAPPED and hollered as Wendell ran home. Lenny had struck out, but in the first game, he'd made it home twice.

My parents were actually here. Ren and her boyfriend.

Brendell. Jen was sitting next to me, scrolling through her phone. My whole family was together.

It was probably a good thing I hadn't heard from Gentry. He wouldn't want to be dumped into this situation. It was too much like bringing a boy home when I was a teenager. The awkward *here's my mom and dad and all my siblings* intro-duction. The only thing Gentry and I had going for us was that he knew all of our names were similar. Darren had nearly pissed himself laughing when I'd made introductions.

Mom leaned closer. "Hey, can you get the boys to driver's ed this summer?"

"Why can't Jen do it?" She had a car. It was the same I used when I was a teen.

Jen rolled her eyes toward me. "Didn't you hear? I'm working at the restaurant. All. Summer."

Ugh. The rite of passage in our family. We had to work at one of the businesses.

"I'd have to see what my schedule's like." Hopefully not wide open like it was now.

"You can always move back home and not worry so much about work," Mom offered.

I didn't tell them that I had paid so far ahead. I didn't want them to think I was Gentry's kept woman. Although, since they worked every second of the day, they might like that idea. "I'm happy where I'm at."

"And you're dating Gentry King?" Mom's tone was more than curious. She actually sounded worried.

"Yes. We've been dating for almost a month."

She dropped her voice. "Is it really dating, honey?"

I bristled. "He's not using me for sex."

She patted my knee. "I'm not saying he is. But he's older and might have different expectations."

Like sex. "We have a lot in common."

The look she gave me said she thought I was deluding

myself. No, I wasn't wealthy and I didn't come from a family with land and a legacy, but I'm sure Gentry did driver's ed runs in his day too.

It was hard to enjoy the rest of the game. I was jobless and dating an older man who wasn't around for me to show off. I blinked back tears. What we had was real. But at times it felt impossible.

"Want to come out with us to eat after the game?"

I warmed at the offer. Using their business to treat us was the only love language Mom and Dad knew. If they were horrible people, it'd be easier to hate them and say no. But they were harried and overwhelmed. And like Brendell said, I enabled them.

"I'll be there."

"Can you bring the twins? Your dad and I will get there early and get the tables arranged."

"Sure, Mom."

The game was like all the others. I cheered on the team, and when it was over, I flagged down Lenny as the rest of our family filtered out.

"You two are riding with me to the restaurant."

He nodded and went back to where his team was gathering around their coach in the outfield.

Wandering out to an open area, my gaze hooked on a tall man striding through the crowd. People parted for him, murmuring to themselves. Even if they didn't know who he was, he walked like he was important.

Gentry's gaze swept the opening, lingering on concessions, then back over, landing on me. His eyes warmed and he changed his trajectory to where I waited by the back of the bleachers. His long, dark coat whipped at his legs like a short cape. With his dark suit and those dark eyes, he made an imposing figure heading my way.

"Hi," I said, giddy beyond belief. He'd come to my little

brother's baseball game. He was here. The guy had an oil company to run, but he was here because I'd asked him.

"Did I miss the game?" He leaned down, but didn't give me a quick peck. His lips softened over mine and he took his time straightening. Anyone that saw would know we were a couple.

"Yes. We won one and lost one. I'm waiting to give the boys a ride."

"How'd they play?" He stepped to my side, willing to stand post with me until the twins came off the field.

"It was their first game, so a little rough. Um…my parents invited me to supper, at their diner. Want to come?" He'd eaten at a diner before, but that was because it was a snow-storm. Then there was Hogan's that served his family's beef. When we hung out at either of our places, we ordered in or cooked. I had no reason to expect him to shun my parents' place, but flutters burst through my belly.

"Sure. Want me to drive?"

"I… They'd have to ride in the back seat." Would he get my meaning?

His eyes crinkled. "And since we haven't christened your car yet, you'd feel better having them in there?"

My face heated. "Yes." He'd said *yet*, and now my mind was going over how we'd position ourselves in the back seat.

Wendell's voice broke through my thoughts, culling my fantasies. "Did you see that catch? I thought for sure I was going to drop—" My brothers rounded the corner and blinked at Gentry.

"Gentry, these are the twins." The boys were easy to tell apart. Wendell was a little taller, and puberty wasn't as kind to his skin. I probably needed to make him a dermatology appointment. "Wendell. Lendell goes by Lenny."

My brothers nodded, their gazes evaluating Gentry from head to toe.

Gentry shook each of their hands. "I hear I missed a good game."

Wendell shrugged, his cheeks going pink. He blushed easily, like me. "I mean, it went all right."

Lenny snickered. "The first one sucked."

We walked to my car and the boys talked over each other about their plays and who messed up and how many base runs they'd have to do at the next practice. Gentry interjected with questions about who else they were playing and where they traveled and if they did summer league. He'd obviously had a son or two in baseball.

I was about to jitter out of my skin by the time we reached the restaurant. Lenny's fingers were fast and furious on his phone. Had he told our parents that Gentry was coming?

All of my siblings were pressed to the window as we weaved through the parking lot. The diner faced the street, but the main entrance was on the side of the parking lot. More than enough windows to spy on us.

"Hey, uh, Kendall." Lenny jogged next to me. "Can you go back to the car with me?"

"Why?" I wasn't going to let Gentry enter this place by himself. He got to the door first and opened it for a couple coming out.

I waited for them to exit, my attention on Gentry, when I heard, "Kendall?"

Darren? What was he doing here? After we got married, he refused to frequent either of my parents' businesses. The girl at his side was the same one from the bedroom. I think. The hair color and the age were the same.

"Hi, Darren." I couldn't sound less thrilled. Gentry let the door close and stood on the other side of Lenny. I was glad this little encounter was taking place outside. The rest of my siblings were still avid spectators in the window.

Darren looked at Lenny. "Hey, Wendell."

Wendell was on the other side of Gentry, half hiding behind him. The kid hated awkwardness as much as me.

My blood pressure notched up. Darren never bothered to learn the difference between the two of them. His disinterest was more insulting than purposely getting it wrong. But I didn't get a chance to correct him.

"This one's Wendell." Gentry tipped his head toward the correct brother, a disapproving frown on his lips. "Clearly."

Darren's eyes narrowed, but there was a spark of recognition. His brow furrowed as if he was figuring out a puzzle. He puffed his chest out farther, but couldn't match up to Gentry's pecs at rest. "You seem to know them so well. Who are you?"

"We just met, actually. But Kendall's told me all about them." Gentry stuck out his hand. "Gentry King."

Darren's face paled. He worked at a refinery owned by King Oil.

I tried, and failed, not to grin. "I thought you didn't like eating here?"

My ex's cheeks fused with color, and he put an arm around his girlfriend. "She wanted to eat here. It's close to where she works."

The woman smiled, but there was rampant curiosity in her eyes. She had no clue this place was owned by her boyfriend's ex-wife's family. I had a feeling that conversation wouldn't go well. She tried to tug him away, but he moved as if his feet were weighed down by concrete blocks.

"So, you two are seeing each other?"

I'd never brought the guy I dated earlier this year around. Darren probably assumed that he was better. "It's still pretty new, but yes."

The girlfriend gave his arm another yank, but Darren

didn't move. "I kick you out and you shack up with the richest guy in the state?" He snorted.

Gentry's face clouds over. He opens his mouth to defend me, but I beat him to it. "No, actually, I have my own place. Gentry hasn't even tried to trick me into living with him." I didn't care to waste my night with Gentry and my family. "Well, we're heading in to eat. See you later."

I breezed past him, and Gentry jumped to get the door for me. I couldn't bite back my grin as I entered and he gave me a little wink.

Lenny rushed up to me. "Kennie, I'm so sorry. When I got the message, I tried to stall you."

Aw. My family wanted to spare me. "Thanks, but it worked out just fine."

Mom rushed to greet me. "He got up to leave as soon as he saw me and your father."

It must've killed Darren to eat here. "No worries, Mom."

The smell of greasy food permeated the air. The place was mostly empty at this time of night, and our table was right in the middle of the main area. We passed the four-foot-high case holding every type of pie you could think of and went toward my family.

The floor was the original white tile with black flecks. *It cleans so nicely, I hate to replace it* was my mom's way of saying they couldn't afford a big remodel. This was the type of place high school and college students worked at and moved on. It kept their turnover and training high. The servers that had been here for years couldn't tolerate the disruption of routines. Things had been done the same way for decades. It was almost a losing battle for my parents, but Dad said the restaurant still paid the mortgage.

My brothers and sisters were openly eyeing Gentry. Lenny and Wendell went right for the table. Their teenage hunger didn't care about any drama, anti-climactic or not.

Dad had a speculative look on his face, and I didn't have to look at Mom to know her expression matched. Gentry showing up would be a big check in his favor.

"Hi everyone. This is Gentry." I gave a lame flourish. If Gentry was looking for sophistication, I was not it.

In his typical fashion, he made his rounds, getting everyone's names and shaking hands. His smile wasn't forced and his laughter was genuine. My chest loosened. When he was done, he pulled out a chair for me.

I gave him a grateful smile and sank into it. Dad planted himself next to Gentry, and Brendell took the seat directly across from him. Dad oozed curiosity while Brendell radiated protective brother vibes.

My heart swelled. This was my family. They took me for granted, but they still cared. I could say no once in a while and they'd continue loving me.

I'd have to give it a shot. But I'd make sure the twins got to driver's ed. The sooner they got a license and a car, the less I'd be pressed to say no. Maybe that was cheating, but I didn't care. I just really loved my family right now.

"I hope you're a burger guy." Dad handed him a menu. I glanced over. Dad's smile was tense. He was embarrassed to be serving the CEO of King Oil greasy burgers.

Gentry's grin was easy and he handed the menu back. "I try to save the caviar for Wednesdays and Friday. Tuesdays are my patty melt and hashbrowns days."

Dad chuckled and Brendell's expression turned from shock to respect.

"I've never had caviar," Brendell said.

"Once was all I needed," Gentry replied. "Fish eggs are a hard sell for a guy who grew up on a beef ranch." The guys laughed, and Dad peppered Gentry with questions about ranching and King's Creek.

Ren elbowed me on my other side. "Hot damn, Kennie," she whispered. "Talk about leveling up."

I grinned, all my anxiety draining away. "I know, right?" We made it through my family's inspection in minutes. His other two sons shouldn't be that big of an obstacle.

entry

I STUDIED the reports in front of me. Printing them off so I could line them up was often easier than switching screens. My environmental advancement team wrote up a giant report on wind power that was making my head spin. I knew oil like the layout of my land, and wind power was easy enough—until the reams of data started.

Sighing, I sat back, bumped my reading glasses up, and rubbed the bridge of my nose. Another Saturday in front of my computer.

But there was one improvement. Kendall hummed to herself in the kitchen. I usually parked myself in my home office for twelve hours each day if I wasn't helping Dawson, but I'd taken up residence with my papers at the kitchen table I never used.

With Kendall, I was back to looking forward to the weekends. Instead of just a change of where I worked, they meant more time with her than a quick supper and grope session.

"I start at my parents' thrift shop tomorrow." She looked over her shoulder as she stirred the pasta sauce. She'd offered to come by and cook a late lunch. I had planned to cook for her, but I had to make sense of these reports and give my investors something to go on. "One of their part-time employees moved away, so I'll be an official employee for a while."

I took my reading glasses off and set them on the table. "How do you feel about that?"

She lifted a shoulder, staring into the pot. "It'll keep me busy. There's only so many jobs in town to apply for. I have an interview next week and I think it'll look better if I say I'm working somewhere even if it's as simple as helping my parents out."

I wanted her to be working with me. But she deserved better than Emilia charging her like a bull protecting its territory. "Good. They'd be schmucks not to hire you."

She glanced at me and smiled, then turned back to the stove. I couldn't quit staring. She wore a baggy pink sweater and black capri leggings that showed her curves better than those boots. Her hair was up in a messy bun and as she stirred the sauce and checked the consistency of the noodles, I had one thought.

I wanted this. I wanted more of this. She'd talk to me about work and I could tell her about mine. We'd eat together and I could touch her instead of daydreaming about it when I had spreadsheets open in front of me.

With my wife, falling in love had been a gradual process. Our future had been planned before we said the big three words to each other. When we said them, we'd meant them but they weren't a big declaration. More like a statement of fact.

This time, I was slammed in the chest with knowing, with yearning, with the realization that I wanted to spend my entire life with this woman. She should know how I felt, but it was too soon. I could just say the words now, but...

We were at different places in our life. She was trying to find a job, and I was keeping a company afloat so hundreds of people weren't jobless. She was pushing thirty, and fifty was around the corner for me.

Twenty years difference. And I still had one son for sure who'd have an insulting opinion about us, and I couldn't expose her to that vitriol. I'd take care of Beckett first. I also had no choice but to accept Xander's silence on the topic as his lack of giving a shit.

But I continued to watch her as she mixed the food together and spread it out in a baking pan that she found God knows where. It'd been so long since I had needed to use it, I would've never remembered where it was. After she slid it into the oven, she set the timer, then faced me. Her cheeks were flushed from the flash of heat from putting the food in to bake. She caught me looking and smiled.

"We have twenty minutes." She slinked over and I was captivated. "Is that enough time for you to get to a stopping point?"

She was about to sit in the chair next to me, but I snagged her hand and drew her onto my lap. Her legs widened to straddle me and I clutched her hips. I'd been hard as a rock since I first saw her ass in those pants.

She rocked over me. "Oh, Mr. King. You've been keeping a secret."

"I have no secrets from you, Ms. Brinkley." And I meant it. I'd tell her everything I was feeling after I called Beckett and told him that this woman was important to me and she'd better get nothing but respect from him.

I slipped her sweater over her head. She wore a lacy bra, a

few shades deeper pink than her top. Tight nipples poked against the fabric.

"You look delicious." I caught one in my mouth. She arched against me, the move crushing her against my erection.

She fisted my white T-shirt in her hands. "Gent. You still have work to finish. We can do this after lunch."

"Fuck my work." I stood, lifting her with me and stretched her out over the table on top of the papers. I wasn't ready to tell her how strongly I felt about her, but I could show her.

I peeled her leggings off. Dear God. Her underwear matched her bra.

I lifted my gaze to hers. "Did you wear these for me?"

"I almost didn't wear any."

With a growl, I rolled them off and tossed them on her pants. Then I parted her thighs and sat back on my chair. Hooking her hips, I jerked her toward me. That earned a sharp inhale, then a sigh as she relaxed her legs open, giving me the best view in the world.

We only had twenty minutes. I had learned everything that made this woman wild. Parting her lips, I flicked my tongue on her clit twice before I devoured her.

Hands twisted in my hair. "Gent—Gentry…" She moaned, her hips bucking into my mouth. She was so responsive, so ready, I added a finger.

"You're going to come fast for me, Kendall. Fast and hard." I went back to work, but it was all pleasure. The way I could elicit moans and make her squirm was powerful.

She did just as I said. Fast. And hard. Her walls clamped around my finger, and I got painfully harder. She'd do that around my cock.

I rose, wiping my face on my shirt as I drew it over my

head. I was prepared to enter her as soon as I was close enough, but I looked down at the last moment.

"Shit. I have to get—"

"Sit." She rolled up and pushed me back. "Take your pants off first, then sit."

I did as she asked, but only because the last of my blood left my head as she unhooked her bra and rolled it down her arms. She held it out and dropped it to the floor.

"You're clean, right?" She straddled me, heat radiating off her.

I nodded. "Always used protection and get my checkups."

"And you've had a vasectomy?"

I nodded again, barely able to look past the tits in front of my face. "Did all the follow-ups to make sure there were no swimmers."

"Then do we need a condom?" She didn't lower herself. She was waiting on me.

This was something I would've never pressured her for, but since she asked, I grabbed her hips. "I want to be as close to you as possible. I want to feel all of you."

I guided her over me, and she sank onto my dick. Her tight heat surrounded me, taking me inch by inch. I had to shut my eyes and lay my forehead on her chest.

"So fucking good." She was wet and hot and velvety. I was going to shame myself by how fast I was going to come, but fuck it. This was amazing.

She started rocking, holding my shoulders. I ran my hands up her bare back and closed my lips around a pebbled nipple.

Licking across it, I blew across the tip. She shuddered and I switched to the other one. As she set a rhythm, I slid a hand between us and teased her clit.

She jerked, her fingers digging in my shoulders. "It's so sensitive."

"Just ride me." I left my hand on her, only her motion causing it to stimulate her.

She tipped her head back, her eyes shut. Then she opened them, her gaze going to the table. She reached for something, but I wasn't coherent enough to notice.

My reading glasses slid onto my face.

"I remember how you didn't want to wear these in the hotel room." She leaned in and nipped at my ear. "So I'm going to come all over you with them on."

I fucking hated my reading glasses, but after this? Maybe they weren't so bad. I nuzzled her neck, nibbling down to her breasts. She rode me faster and I barely held on, finally feeling the ripples go through her as her body clenched.

She cried out. I gritted my teeth and let my climax slam home.

Ecstasy poured through me. We were skin to skin. The glasses felt like a clear signal that I wasn't close to her age, but she still wanted me.

This woman was it for me. She was my forever.

GETTING ready the next morning had a welcome sense of familiarity. I was going to go for a run, but Kendall was heading out to get some fresh air on the walking paths near my place. So I walked with her.

Then we showered together. The higher water bill was worth it.

Today, I made her a quick lunch, determined to be the one to feed her before she left for work.

My papers from yesterday were stacked on the table. I'd read through some other market analyses reports.

She came out, fresh from her shower—her real shower— and sat at the table. She wore the same pink sweater, but it was paired with jeans that hugged her in all the right places. "Wind power. Mind if I take a peek?"

"Go for it. It's enough to put me to sleep."

I hadn't realized how sad my grocery situation was in the house. Reheated pasta coming right up. I added more cheese and tossed it in the oven.

While she read, I leaned against the counter. Her forehead was puckered, but her eyes rapidly scanned the page.

"Wow. I didn't realize the cost that went into wind power."

"Not many do. Not even our investors. But they want companies like mine to make sure our capital investment goes toward processes with lower carbon emissions. And people are just as willing to have a giant windmill on their land as they are an oil well." Which was to say, not that thrilled. "Sometimes the backlash from neighbors makes it feel like it's not worth it."

She ran her finger down the page, her mouth working over the data. "I can already see how you can compare the expense of a mill versus a well and how long it'll take to pay off."

I nodded. "They each have their own advantage, and they each have major disadvantages, both with cost and climate. But it doesn't do to put it in my language. The investors need it in theirs. At least I speak it better than Emilia."

"You should have someone who didn't grow up oil but knows the business write it instead."

"I agree. Aiden's got too much to do, so this is what I do on weekends."

She sighed wistfully and tapped her forehead. "The report is already forming up here." She rattled off how she'd start it and then put it in layman's terms that wasn't insulting the investors intelligence. Pure facts, but with personality. Something Aiden and I struggled with.

"I could use you on the team." I needed to have a long talk with Emilia.

"Maybe in another life, right?"

Maybe not, but I had to do some checking first. I didn't want to shove another job at her that she didn't want but was in a position where she couldn't say no. Besides, it'd take some work with Emilia.

As we ate, she read over the rest and we chatted about how I should present the information. Her style was so out of my comfort zone. I would usually pick out the highlights of the report, run a few numbers, and there they had it. Aiden would roll his eyes, but since the meetings were in person, I could talk through everything else.

I was walking her to her car when another familiar car drove up. A stern face glared at me from the window.

Emilia.

Kendall stiffened next to me. We stopped on the edge of the sidewalk. I should've had her park in the garage, but the weather was nice and I didn't care who knew she was here.

Emilia got out, her eyes narrowed on my hand on Kendall's back. "What the hell, Gentry?"

"Emilia."

"I told you to be done with her."

I cocked my head. "Excuse me. You told her to quit, and she *chose* to."

"That didn't mean you should keep sleeping with her." She crossed her arms. It was Sunday, but she was dressed like she was heading to a board meeting right after this. Red power-suit and heels. "Aiden let slip that she was helping you out in the office. You know the rules."

"It's your policy that no one agrees with," I said calmly.

I didn't have to look at Kendall's hands to know she was white-knuckling her overnight bag. I kept my hand on her back.

Emilia jabbed a finger toward her. "She got a job at King Oil. She got into the inner office. Now she's here." She gave me a *how stupid are you* look. "Did she offer to help you with work while she was here?"

"Ms. Boyd." Unfortunately, Kendall sounded guilty as hell.

"She has some valuable insight," I said.

"I'll bet it's her *insight* that got her access to your secure information." Emilia turned her glare to Kendall, looking like an eagle ready to puncture a rodent with its beak. "You need to stop sleeping with him and forget King Oil. Forget Gentry. I don't know how I ever thought you'd be good for my grandson. I wish I could go back in time. Have some self-respect and go after someone your own age."

With the way Emilia scared her off before, I was afraid her sheer meanness was all it'd take. "Emilia—"

"I have to go." Kendall skittered out of my reach to her vehicle.

"Kendall," I took a step after her.

"Gentry. You've always needed me to clean up your messes."

That statement got through the upset she'd caused showing up here. I had enough. Before Kendall got into her car, I called to her. "I'll call you tonight."

She looked at me, then at Emilia. Her gaze darted away and she drove off. Maybe I should've dealt with this while Kendall was here, but I had a feeling Emilia would listen better one on one.

When I turned back to Emilia, her gloating expression only raised my blood pressure. She opened her mouth to speak, but I talked over her. "Let's go inside."

"I've done all I needed to here. I heard she was still clinging to you and when I saw her car I knew I had to stop." She turned her back on me.

Which meant she'd probably been driving by often *looking*

for Kendall's car. "Emilia," I snapped. "Get the fuck inside. We're going to talk."

Her shoulders went rigid and she slowly turned around. I'd never spoken to her that way.

I let her lead. When we were in and she was seated on the couch I hardly used in the living room, I sat across from her.

I looked her in the eye and said, "I'm not letting her go and it's none of your business."

"Do I need to remind you that your job—"

"Is my job. Fire me. Or don't. But you don't get a say about Kendall. If you don't want her touching King Oil business, fine, but it's your loss. She's really good at understanding information, and I think the investors would love her. We all know what a hard time they have with you."

Her jaw went tight and she looked away. Rebranding the company hadn't been enough all those years ago. Emilia and DB had nearly run the company into the ground, and we did a major overhaul. Along with the name change and my promotion to CEO, we'd moved headquarters to Billings. She still had power, but there was enough buffer to keep her influence from being completely negative.

"And know that if you fire me, you're hurting Aiden."

She sucked in a breath and seemed to consider what I was saying. "Aiden's a big boy and more than capable of taking over."

It wasn't a job for one guy. Hell, it wasn't a job for two guys, but I let that matter drop. "Then fire me, Emilia. But if you ever talk to Kendall like that again, we are done. We are *fucking* done."

She recoiled, putting her hand on her heart. "Gentry—"

"And you will apologize."

Her hand slipped down and she peered at me. "She's really gotten to you."

"She couldn't care less whether she works at King Oil or

not. She just wants to work, and bonus if she enjoys the job. But I'm the lucky bastard she cares about—despite the way Beckett spoke to her over the phone and how you treat her. She's not with me for my money, and I don't care one fuck who believes that."

"But she's so young. What if she wants kids, what if she wants—"

"Still not your business. I know what she wants and she knows what I want." I held her gaze. "I loved Sarah. You know that. It's why you didn't care if I slept around after her death. As long as they didn't get near my heart—or near the company—you didn't care. Kendall's done both and you're scared."

Emilia's eyes misted over and she looked away, her chin lifted. "First, I lost Sarah. Then I lost DB. I'm not losing this company."

Never mind losing me, but Emilia wasn't one to show emotion to anyone. I often thought she pointed DB out of a crowd and said, "You. We're getting married," and that was that.

"It's all I have." She waved at me. "You have your own life, but as long as you had no life, you were dedicated to the company."

"You have four grandkids."

She scoffed. "Four grown men have no use for a grandma. It's not like I've knitted a single stitch in my entire life to give them each a hat to remember me by."

"Remember that before you drive them away with your trust talk."

"It's hundreds of millions of dollars, Gentry."

"It's your grandsons."

"It's all I have to leave them." She sniffled and looked away again.

Ah. I should've guessed. Just like I figured out why

Kendall bothered Emilia so badly, I should've seen behind her motivations with the trusts. It was still about her animosity with the Cartwrights, but it was also all she knew to pass on. She didn't sew, or knit, or have any other trade or treasured item to pass down. She had money. And Sarah had tied it up out of her reach. Probably for the very reason the Boyds made all that money in the first place. First, they screwed over their friends selling them land they suspected had oil, and then used their mineral rights to make millions.

Emilia tapped her fingers on her thigh. "You really like this girl?"

"I'm in love with her." I would've liked to have told Kendall first, but it needed to be done this way. Emilia needed to know how serious I was.

"You never said that when I asked you how you felt about Sarah that day."

I remembered. I'd said that I care about her and would do what's right. The love came later and it was still there. "I miss her, Emilia. Every day. Don't ever doubt it. We loved each other and she was my best friend. But it was a lifetime ago. Kendall is my now. She's my future. And I think you'd find she could be good for the company's future."

There was that proud lift of her chin. "I'll think about it."

I grinned. "Think all you want. You're still going to apologize."

endall

MY EYES WERE scratchy from crying, and my throat was raw. I was at work today, wearing the same thing I had on yesterday when I left Gentry's. I'd stayed at my parents and ignored his calls and messages. Had he stopped by my apartment?

He could've probably figured out where my parents lived, but he respected my wishes. His last message said, *Please call me when you're ready.*

Emilia hated me. She thought I was a deceitful mistress, and after a lifetime of people pleasing, it bothered me on a level I couldn't begin to understand. I didn't even know her. Why did I care?

"That'll be two fourteen, please." I bagged up the T-shirts. Mondays were dollar shirt day. I had barely needed any training. The days of working here through college came roaring back.

I hadn't made it any farther now that I had then. I'd finished my education. No job. And I was still running my siblings all over town.

Shoppers were milling around, but no one was at the till. I dug out a rag and the Windex and starting polishing off the conglomeration of fingerprints that had built up on the display glass over the weekend.

"Where can I find Kendall Brinkley?" The deep voice behind was eerily familiar, but it wasn't Gentry.

I straightened and looked up. Familiar dark eyes, a stern face much like his brother's, and seething hatred in his eyes.

Beckett. The angry voice on the phone in Douglas.

I sighed and set the rag down. "Hi, Beckett. I'm Kendall."

"You know who I am?"

"Obviously, you're a regular here."

He frowned and I wanted to giggle. The freedom of my sarcastic remark was intoxicating. He was wearing a suit that probably cost more than what I'd make in a year working both the thrift store and the diner.

"We need to talk."

We really didn't, but my urge to fight was drained. Catty comments were all I had after a shitty night's sleep in my old bed. I looked around the store and found the only other employee on today. "Gladys, can you take over for me for a bit?"

"Sure." The older woman zoomed around a rack and stopped when she saw Beckett. She glanced from him to me.

I just said "thanks" and headed for the back office, not caring if he followed. From the faces popping up like prairie dogs tracking my progress, he was right behind me.

I stepped into the office but didn't shut the door. I didn't care if the world heard my drama. It might be good for business.

I didn't sit, but folded my arms and faced him. Like the

others, I could pick out what traits were from him and what must come from his mother. Like his brothers, he strongly resembled his dad. His mannerisms were probably from Sarah, though I had yet to see him as anything but pissed.

"What business do you have with my dad?"

Seriously? "I don't think you're old enough to hear it."

He jerked like he couldn't believe I'd made the joke. I couldn't either, but it was invigorating. "Do you think this is funny? You targeted my dad for his money, for his—"

I put a hand up and closed my eyes. Surprised it actually worked, I took a steadying breath. "Look. I've had *a day* that started yesterday when your grandma chewed me out and called me a traitorous gold digger. I don't care to hear those accusations again. You have a grudge against your dad, for good reason, I understand." I shrugged. "Though *you* don't understand."

"What the hell don't I understand?"

I really should butt right out, but this might be the last time I ever had to interact with him so I didn't care. "That your dad had no one to turn to. That he sought out temporary relief for lasting pain. That he let no one in, but somehow I got in over a game of Scrabble. Or it might have been War. Maybe gin rummy."

His brows dropped. "What?"

"In the hotel, he wanted nothing to do with me, but the power went out. So we played cards and board games. It gave us a lot of time to get to know each other."

"My dad? Played games?"

"Yep."

Beck's upper lip curled. "What else did you do?"

"Not what I wanted. He stopped it at a kiss. Then we flew home and went our separate ways."

He shook his head. "You worked at—"

"He got me the job. I didn't ask for it." I rubbed my

temples. "And I'm so grateful for that storm. I never would've tolerated working for you."

"I never would've hired you."

"And I never would've hit on you. Boys aren't my type."

His look turned incredulous. "Boys?"

I put my hands on my hips, almost done with this conversation. "Guys who haven't grown up. Guys who use their girlfriends or wives as tools for convenience. Guys who blame others for why they're not where they want to be in life. I've been there. Have the ex-husband with the college girlfriend to prove it. I'm done. And honestly, I'm done with your dad too. If he tolerates your grandmother dictating my life—and his—nope. Done."

I huffed out a breath. That was so freeing. I gave up a marriage because Darren made me choose between him and my family. Then I let him sweet talk me into staying in the house, just so he could end up kicking me out when it suited him. I'd fallen for Gentry because he was the opposite of Darren—ambitious, confident, and secure. But I gave up so much time with him because of what Ms. Boyd might do, or what his kids might think. And then I caved to what they wanted me to do in the end.

I wanted to work and be the best big sister ever. That was what I would do—single or not. "Now, if you'll excuse me. I'm helping my parents out. Feel free to check out the dollar day T-shirt rack."

I stormed out of the office. Gladys was behind the counter, a stunned gaze directed at the front door. An imposing figure stood in the entry.

I stopped. "Gentry. What are you doing here?"

I don't know how, but my feet moved again. Gladys leaned forward and whispered, "Are we having a deal on hot men in suits?"

A nervous giggle escaped. I wasn't exactly quiet. The

whole store probably heard my conversation. What had he heard?

He didn't smile when he saw me. So that answered what he'd heard. His grim gaze lifted to look behind me and his jaw flexed. "Beckett."

"Dad."

"The dollar deal rack is over there." I started for the counter.

"Emilia should be contacting you with an apology." Gentry's words stopped me again. "And after I talk with Beckett, he'll apologize as well."

"Dad—"

"Beckett, enough. I told your grams how it was going to be last night, and I'll tell you. If Kendall still wants to be with me after all this BS, then we are no one's business. Not your grams. Not you. Not your brothers."

Had he really talked to Ms. Boyd? About us? I chanced a look at Beckett. He was staring at his dad like he'd never seen him before.

"You told Grams off?" He was stunned. Possibly more than I was. Made sense. He'd grown up around the woman.

"I did. She's wrong about Kendall, as are you." Gentry's expression softened and he walked toward me. The spectacle we were creating mattered less the closer he got.

He caressed my face. "I'm sorry."

I swallowed. "I thought you—"

"Would do nothing about Emilia like I've always done? I don't blame you." He kissed my forehead. "I'm sorry. About all of this."

"We knew it was coming."

"I should've taken care of it before it happened." He tugged me into him. "Don't be done with me. I have a lot more to offer."

I gave him a little smile. "You still have to teach me Canasta."

He was about to kiss me when Beck appeared at our side. "Kendall, if I'm wrong about you, then I will apologize."

Gentry's hold on me tightened like he was afraid I'd storm off again. "Beckett, that wasn't an apology."

"No," I said. "It's okay. He needs time before he can trust me. I just want to be treated with respect."

Beck dipped his head. "You will have that." He slid his gaze to his dad. "Did you really? With Grams?"

The corner of Gentry's mouth lifted. "I even swore at her."

Beck's brows lifted, then he turned serious again. "Your...*girlfriend*...said something. About finding temporary relief for lasting pain. It doesn't change how I feel about everything, but I'll try to understand better."

Gentry released me to put his hand on Beck's shoulder. "That's more than I expected. None of it ever changed how things were before your mom died."

Beck nodded, his throat working as he turned and strode out of the store. The guy hadn't gotten over the death of his mom. I hope he found closure someday soon.

Gentry didn't let me go. "I think we created a scene."

Gladys piped up. "I don't mind."

I giggled and buried my face in Gentry's suit. "I don't even know what to think right now."

"I love you, Kendall."

I jerked my head up. Had I heard right?

"I was going to wait until I set Emilia and Beckett straight before I told you, but I shouldn't have waited. You might've had more faith in me."

I wanted to ride the high, but he had one more son who hadn't met me. "What about Xander?"

Gentry took his phone out and punched in a number. It rang and rang. He punched it in again. Same thing. He tried again. This time, I heard a distant voice pick up.

"Yeah?"

"Xander. I've met someone. She's twenty years younger than me, and if she wants to come work with me, she'll get access to the inner office. Does that bother you?"

Xander's voice was clear. "Should it?"

"No."

"Okay, then." He was still huffing like he was walking or hiking. "Beck giving you issues?"

"Not anymore."

"Grams."

"No longer a problem."

A laugh. "Good luck with that."

Fatherly concern entered Gentry's eyes. "Where are you?"

"Sri Lanka."

Whoa. Just wandering the world.

"Have fun. Be safe." Gentry's voice grew stern and holy crap did that get to me. My belly fluttered. "Call once in a while."

"Right. Take care, Dad." Xander disconnected.

"You worry about him."

"A lot." Gentry slipped his phone into his pocket and looked around the store. We were standing in the middle. Shoppers were checking out, but watching us as they did. "I should let you go back to work."

"What'd you mean by the inner office thing?"

"Emilia will come around. I mean it Kendall. I think you'd make a great addition."

"Everyone will think I got the job because I'm sleeping with you."

He lifted a shoulder. "I only care if you care. But I do care that you take your time deciding. I support whatever you decide"

Did I? I scanned the store. I'd just made the biggest spectacle of my life and wasn't bothered a bit.

"No. I don't care. Because I love you too."

entry

CONCENTRATING on the report in front of me was an impossible task. I listened for the corner office door to open and close. Footsteps coming my way. I'd never been as tense for a meeting as I was now.

The minutes ticked by and while I usually like reading the reports of a new drilling site, today it was tedious.

Were they done?

Finally, I heard a voice drift through the top floor. The voices faded and light heels clicked closer to my office.

There was a light knock and Kendall opened the door. My office had nice aesthetic, but it was nothing like seeing Kendall walk in. Her hair was secured in a chignon and she wore my favorite boots with leggings and a sundress. Her cardigan fought off the chill of the AC and gave her a more formal look.

She closed the door behind her.

My work was forgotten. "How'd it go?"

"They felt really bad for what they did."

"They should." I had talked to Mrs. Chan about the way her team welcomed Kendall and then ditched her. I should've done it earlier. Once Kendall had gotten settled, I didn't miss how nervous she was about running across her old coworkers. We needed to clear the air and find out of the whole thing had been a setup, a trap, or both.

Her grin was indulgent. "It was a setup yes, but they wanted us to end up together. It wasn't done maliciously they said."

"That's their story and they're sticking to it?"

She sank into the chair across from my desk. "I told them that it worked. If it wasn't for them, we might have ignored how we felt. And I wanted them to know that just because I was in the inner office, the policy of not being stupid still applies to me. Ms. Boyd will make sure of it."

My tension eased. Kendall had a way of winning over everyone. Emilia came to see her more than she did me. She learned Kendall likes talking shop way more than I do, and they would often be lost talking hypotheticals about the business for hours.

But it didn't stop Emilia from mentioning that if Beckett doesn't secure his trust, Kendall and I may both have our walking papers. I suspected she gave way to Kendall so easy to give herself leverage. I might step down over her threats over Beckett getting married, but Emilia knew that I'd weather a lot to keep her force from impacting Kendall.

Working at King Oil with the major stressor that was Emilia Boyd wouldn't be the same if she suddenly grew a conscience and stricter morals.

Kendall made it more tolerable. "Are you all packed for after work?"

"Yes. Fourth of July fireworks in Denver. I can't wait." She stretched. "Want to break for a walk?"

"You go. I have a meeting at noon."

She got me away from the desk more than ever but it wasn't always possible.

"I'll bring you lunch, then." She blew me a kiss and sauntered out.

I couldn't wait for the trip. We were going to have supper with Beckett and then Kendall and I would watch fireworks from our room. Naked.

And I had one important question to ask her.

"THIS PLACE IS SO FANCY," Kendall whispered.

We were at a fine dining establishment specializing in Piemontese fare. The table cloths were white, the waiters were proper, and the food was expensive. I'd been to enough of these restaurants, but experiencing it through Kendall's eyes was like a first for me each time.

Beckett gave her a bemused look. My son softened toward her each time we met up. Slowly, our father-son relationship was repairing itself. Anger no longer rolled off him in waves when we spoke. There was still progress to make, but I had a feeling it had to do with losing his mother more than with me.

That was something he'd have to work out. My job was to make sure he felt comfortable talking to me whenever he needed to.

Our food had come and gone. The evening was winding down and the fireworks would start soon.

"What are your plans for the evening?" Kendall asked Beckett.

"I'm heading home. Since you have the plane here and are

staying for a few days, I'm flying out to Atlanta to talk to a prospective client."

"On the holiday weekend?" I asked. Would I have thought twice about working over the Fourth of July before Kendall? I knew the answer.

He shrugged. "He's the one that wants the money for backing."

"If you'll excuse me." Kendall slipped out and went in the direction of the restroom. Her cocktail dress hugged her ass. I couldn't wait to take it off.

Beckett interrupted my leering. "You two are really something."

"What do you mean?"

"I feel like I'm dining with a teenage couple. But you're my dad. It's weird."

"It is for me too." I swirled my wineglass. "I'm happy, Beckett. Really happy."

"Good. I wish Aiden loosened up like you when he got married."

"Me too." That dulled my evening a little, but that was parenthood. The underlying worry for my kids was always there.

"Has your grams tracked you down?"

He blew out a breath. "I'm training in the new recruit she sent my way, but I have no plans to date her. It's...rough. Grams is getting more desperate."

My son came off as a hard ass, but he was too polite to turn away the people Emilia sent his way. He always gave them a chance at the job. I think he felt bad that Emilia wasted their time. "You have a little over six months, Beckett. You can make it. And maybe even meet someone."

His quiet grunt was the end of the subject.

Kendall was on her way back to the table. Beckett and I rose. His driver was waiting for us.

We were dropped off at the hotel. Kendall strutted into our room and let her hair down as soon as I closed the door.

I held her hand and drew her toward the floor-to-ceiling window. We were on the top floor and would have a nice view. But I had one thing to get out of the way first.

I reached into my pocket. She was still looking out the window when I took her hands. Turning toward me, there was a delicate arch to her brows.

I was about to drop to one knee when her phone rang. She grimaced but didn't go for her phone.

"Go ahead," I urged. It was our thing. I didn't worry that I was a priority, and she was mine, which included her loved ones.

She slipped her phone out of her pocket. "Hello? Your car's not working? No, I can't give you a ride. I'm out of town. Denver. Yes. *Stop it*, Jen." Her cheeks flushed. "Have fun, but not too much." She hung up. "She wants to go to a friend's cabin, but Mom won't let her drive that far."

With that out of the way, I took her hand again.

And her phone rang. This time when she answered it, she said, "Hey, I'll call you when I get back to town. Gentry took me on a getaway and I'm shutting my phone off." She grinned and hung up. "Jen said she doesn't want to know what she's interrupting."

She shut her phone down and tossed it on the bed. It was a common occurrence now. She decided her own boundaries but continued to be active in their lives.

At last, there was no more waiting. I dropped to one knee. Her eyes widened.

"I never got to this before," I said as my knee hit the floor. Her mouth dropped open and her eyes glittered.

Opening the box with a twinkling square diamond ring that I knew without asking would be her style, I gazed up at the woman I wanted to spend the rest of my life with.

"Kendall Brinkley, will you marry me?" My lungs stopped working as I waited for her answer.

She pressed a hand to her chest, the other waving in front of her face. "Yes. Oh my God, *yes!*"

I wanted to gather her into my arms, but I tugged the ring free and slipped it on her shaking finger.

She held her hand out. "I love it." When she looked at me, her face was full of emotion. "But I love you more, Gent."

Gent had become my pet name. Since she was the only one who ever shortened my name like that, I never tired of hearing it.

I rose, grateful there was no creaking or popping from my joints. "And I love you, Ms. Brinkley."

Heat infused her eyes and she slid her hands over my shoulders.

I gripped her fingers. "After the fireworks, I'm going to ravish you, but I don't want you to miss this." Her smile was exactly what I wanted to wake up to every morning.

I pulled up the chair and settled her on my lap as we faced the window. The day I told Emilia that Kendall was my present and my future, I'd meant every word. No matter what that woman tossed our way, I would get through it with Kendall at my side. She was my partner, my best friend, and the love of my life.

CHAPTER 23

eck

THE SUN SHONE over the fading green of the lawn and the multitude of flowers Dawson had planted to make the flowerbeds look good for Dad's wedding were still blooming this early in October.

Give 'em a week. Between me and the weather, they won't last, he'd said with a grin. He could keep hundreds of head of cattle alive, but not a mum to save his life.

My childhood home had been done up on a smaller scale than Aiden's wedding last year, with only enough chairs for our family and Kendall's. I glanced to where he sat with Kate. She was beaming at Kendall and Dad. My stepmother and my dad. How weird was that? Kendall was only a year older than me.

But the way she'd told me off had come from someone with a far older soul. She'd been dealing with some stuff and I'd hit the last peg of her tolerance.

Oddly, it was her tirade that had made me think that maybe what her and Dad had was real. Then Aiden told me about Dad and Grams. Dad never stood up to her. There was too much history, and with Aiden a major part of the company, too much on the line if Grams made one of her impulsive decisions, like she did in the corn ethanol days.

It finally got through to me that Kendall was different in all the right ways.

I looked around. Dad and Kendall were strolling down the lawn between the chairs, hanging onto each other and looking like the newlyweds they were, which I guess one of them was. Dad hadn't worn a suit. At Kendall's request, he was in his black dress jeans from years ago, a crisp white shirt, and his boots. The cowboy hat he wore was the good one he'd left at the house. Kendall wore a simple white sleeveless smock dress and sandals.

They looked good together.

My resentment toward Dad eased a little more. I hadn't noticed how stern he'd looked for the last few years. I glanced at Aiden. The role of overworked fun-sucker now went to my oldest brother.

Xander leaned over and whispered, "She's after you."

Grams's silver bob was turning this way and that, looking for me. Why was she looking for me when I was surrounded by my dad, his new wife, and three of my brothers?

Because I was the next to turn twenty-nine.

We filed out of the row, Dawson and I going to help man the grill to feed the crowd. I rushed in front of him, hoping he'd block me. Dawson shifted to the side.

"Bastard," I muttered over my shoulder.

He laughed and beckoned Brendell over. Anyone who had grill skills was cooking. Kendall's sister Ren had baked the wedding cake and was taking pictures of it for her new bakery business's brochure.

Kendall had broken off from Dad, heading toward her sister.

Dawson called to her. "Did I hear right? Your honeymoon is in *Douglas, Wyoming?*"

Her face lit up with excitement. "Going back to where it all started, then we're heading to Broadway. I was just going to tell my sister that the lady who sheltered us from the storm runs a bakery and I could talk to her."

Ren looked over. "You'll talk to her for me? On your *honeymoon?*"

"Her name's Gale, and I'm sure she'd be happy to share the secrets of her success." Kendall's gaze landed on Dad and went downright sappy. "Excuse me." She rushed off.

I was about to steal a cupcake, not realizing Dawson had ditched me when Grams's voice cut in.

"Did you ever find anyone to fill your opening?"

Abandoning the sweets, I turned. I knew she was talking about the opening as my significant other and not the executive assistant opening. I was only talking about the one. My love life was off-limits.

"As a matter of fact, yes."

A shrewd look enhanced the green in her hazel eyes. "How are you two getting along?'

Oh, hell. Grams was behind this applicant too? She was getting sneakier about how she'd send prospective applicants my way. I was glad Kendall had been waylaid by the storm. I couldn't turn them down because of all people, I understood the force that was Grams. And I needed an assistant.

But now that I thought of it, my new hire wore tight revealing clothing. Not that I usually cared. I wasn't out to sleep with my employees, and women should be able to wear what they want without being judged. I could show up in board shorts and a tank and people would just think I'm an eccentric millionaire who owned a tech company.

But my new assistant also insisted on business lunches and brought a bag to work in case we had to fly somewhere on short notice. I often did and hadn't thought too hard about it. But if Grams had filled her ear with how lonely I was and how badly I needed a wife and how much money I had and would have if I got married…

Fuck. I picked up a glass of punch and sipped it on my way to the grill. Dawson already had his apron on and nice flames going.

"Grams sent my new assistant my way. I thought it was a legitimate applicant this time."

"You're off your game."

"Yeah. But seriously, it can't be that hard to find an assistant who doesn't want to sleep with me, who understands the gaming and app world, and doesn't care how much money I have and wants to actually do the job."

Dawson looked over to where Grams chatted with Kendall's parents. "There are. But they have to beat the ones Grams sends your way."

Yeah. If this assistant quit on me, I'd be ready for the next one she shoved in my direction.

————

BECKETT MIGHT BE ready for what Grams has in mind, but he's not ready for who shows up at his office in King's Ransom.

GET YOUR BONUS EPILOGUE HERE!

. . .

THANK YOU FOR READING. I'd love to know what you thought. Please consider leaving a review for King's Crown at the retailer the book was purchased from.

FOR ALL THE LATEST NEWS, sneak peeks, quarterly short stories, and free material sign up for my newsletter.

ABOUT THE AUTHOR

Marie Johnston writes paranormal and contemporary romance and has collected several awards in both genres. Before she was a writer, she was a microbiologist. Depending on the situation, she can be oddly unconcerned about germs or weirdly phobic. She's also a licensed medical technician and has worked as a public health microbiologist and as a lab tech in hospital and clinic labs. Marie's been a volunteer EMT, a college instructor, a security guard, a phlebotomist, a hotel clerk, and a coffee pourer in a bingo hall. All fodder for a writer!! She has four kids, an old cat, and a puppy that's bigger than half her kids.

mariejohnstonwriter.com

Follow me:

Printed in Great Britain
by Amazon